LILY & KOSMO

IN *OUTER OUTER SPACE*

LILY & KOSMO
IN OUTER OUTER SPACE

Written and Illustrated by
JONATHAN ASHLEY

SIMON & SCHUSTER BOOKS FOR YOUNG READERS
NEW YORK   LONDON   TORONTO   SYDNEY   NEW DELHI

SIMON & SCHUSTER BOOKS FOR YOUNG READERS
An imprint of Simon & Schuster Children's Publishing Division
1230 Avenue of the Americas, New York, New York 10020
This book is a work of fiction. Any references to historical events, real people, or real places
are used fictitiously. Other names, characters, places, and events are products of the author's
imagination, and any resemblance to actual events or places or persons, living or dead,
is entirely coincidental.
Copyright © 2018 by Jonathan Ashley
All rights reserved, including the right of reproduction in whole or in part in any form.
SIMON & SCHUSTER BOOKS FOR YOUNG READERS is a trademark of
Simon & Schuster, Inc.
For information about special discounts for bulk purchases, please contact
Simon & Schuster Special Sales at 1-866-506-1949 or business@simonandschuster.com.
The Simon & Schuster Speakers Bureau can bring authors to your live event. For more
information or to book an event, contact the Simon & Schuster Speakers Bureau at
1-866-248-3049 or visit our website at www.simonspeakers.com.
Book design by Krista Vossen
The text for this book was set in Fournier.
The illustrations for this book were rendered digitally, in pen and ink.
Manufactured in the United States of America
First Edition
2 4 6 8 10 9 7 5 3 1
Library of Congress Cataloging-in-Publication Data
Names: Ashley, Jonathan, author.
Title: Lily & Kosmo in outer outer space / Jonathan Ashley.
Other titles: Lily and Kosmo
Description: First edition. | New York : Simon & Schuster Books for Young Readers, [2018]
| Summary: Lily Lupino yearns to be an astronaut, so when Kosmo Kidd crash-lands in her
Brooklyn kitchen in 1949, she will do almost anything to prove herself to him and his crew.
Identifiers: LCCN 2017042020 | ISBN 9781534413641 (hardcover)
| ISBN 9781534413665 (eBook)
Subjects: | CYAC: Astronauts—Fiction. | Space flight—Fiction. | Brothers and sisters—
Fiction. | Sex role—Fiction. | Humorous stories. Classification: LCC PZ7.1.A84 Lil 2018 |
DDC [Fic]—dc23
LC record available at https://lccn.loc.gov/2017042020

For Meghan and Dorothy
Whatever smiles this book may bring originated with you

CHAPTER 1

Brooklyn, Earth, 1949

The night Lily Lupino locked herself in the bathroom and cut off all her hair, a piece of space crash landed in her living room, in the form of a boy astronaut named Kosmo Kidd. He came by rocket, a small beat-up number that smashed through the ceiling while the Lupinos slept—well, not Lily. Lily was too mad to sleep. It started with a radio, looming over the living room like a cherrywood lighthouse, and the whine of a theremin, announcing the start of tonight's episode of *Trip Darrow: Star Pilot. . . .*

Mr. Lupino was done listening to the evening news, and Mrs. Lupino's favorite music program, *Bandstand*, didn't come on until eight. Seven p.m. belonged to Lily Lupino, Astronaut in Training. For the fifth Thursday in a row, she sat cross-legged on the carpet, in the amber glow of the radio's dial, grabbed the knob, and tuned in to join the baritone spaceman Trip Darrow, and his squeaky sidekick, Deirdre. Tonight, the five-part epic

"Mutants on Moon Base Four" would reach its thrilling conclusion.

Lily took off her horn-rimmed glasses, let the living room dissolve into a blur . . .

The opening theremin music faded, and the story picked up right where it had left off last week, with Trip and Deirdre hiking across an alien moon, in search of the missing chemist Dr. Wyndecott. Their footsteps thumped through moondust. Their metal space gear clinked with every step. Their voices echoed inside their helmets. . . .

> TRIP: *Activate the Vita-Scanner, Deirdre! On a barren moon like this, even the smallest blip should lead us straight to Dr. Wyndecott's lab.*

> DEIRDRE: *Golly, Mr. Darrow, do you really suppose the doc's air supply coulda held out this long?*

> TRIP: *It's not his lungs I'm worried about, but his very soul.*

Deirdre's Vita-Scanner *blipped* faster and faster. The hum of the theremin rose to a desperate pitch. . . .

> DEIRDRE: *Mr. Darrow, look! The doc's lab!*

There's a light on, and . . . And there's the doc, locked inside the Morpho-Sphere!

TRIP: Alive?

Tak-tak-tak-tak-tak. A clash of cymbals drowned out the radio, and Lily turned to see two piggish eyes smiling at her from under the sofa. It was Alfie, her two-year-old brother, with his windup velveteen pig-soldier, Colonel Shanks.

"I can't hear!" Lily shouted, and cranked up the knob.

DEIRDRE: Sure, he's alive all right, but . . . but he's . . . changing. . . .

TRIP: Yes, Deirdre, mutating. Before our very eyes!

"Can it in there! I'm on the telephone," growled Mr. Lupino in his study, covering the receiver, and coughing pipe smoke. Actually, to call it a "study" isn't quite right, more of a nook between the coatrack and the broom closet. But there was room for a desk, a desk lamp, a telephone, a high-backed leather chair, and a pipe tray. And that was all Mr. Lupino needed—well, that and a little quiet. "You hear me? Quiet, I said!"

"Okay!" said Lily. "I'm turning it down."

"No, not *down*. Off."

"Off?" cried Lily. "But it's the conclusion!"

"Lily, sweetie!" called Mrs. Lupino from the kitchen. Her scalp was pulled tight with curlers, her brain was adrift in show tunes, and her hands were drowning in dish suds. "You heard your father. Radio off!"

"Fine," groaned Lily. But when she turned the knob, she stopped just short of off, leaving just enough signal that she could hear it if she leaned in close. . . .

TRIP: I'm afraid we're too late, Deirdre. The serum's already taken hold. The doc . . . he's completely—

5

Tak-tak-tak-tak-tak. The clatter of cymbals pounded straight into Lily's eardrum, and she turned to find Alfie giggling, holding Colonel Shanks next to her head. She snatched the pig, and sat on it. Alfie pushed and poked, but Lily wouldn't budge. He got hold of one of the Colonel's legs, and tugged with all his might. Stitches popped, and Alfie toppled to the floor, holding the cleanly ripped-off velveteen leg. Tears filled his eyes, his mouth gaped, and he began to wail.

"Shush!" Lily yelled, pressing one ear to the warm speaker, and covering the other with her palm. She shut her eyes. If she hadn't, she might have seen Mr. Lupino glaring at her through a veil of pipe smoke, his face turning red as a fire engine. . . .

DEIRDRE: His face! He—he ain't human!

TRIP: Mercy, Deirdre! He's seen us!

And if she weren't so close to the speaker, she might have heard the familiar squeak of Mr. Lupino's chair as he stood up, and the floorboards creaking as he marched across the floor. . . .

TRIP: Fear not, Deirdre! My Dissolve-O-Ray will make fast work of that fiend.

DEIRDRE: Rats, Mr. Darrow! Now I've gone and done it: I forgot to charge that Dissolve-O-Thingy. Can you ever forgive me?

TRIP: The fault is mine, Deirdre. A barren moon like this is no place for a simple Earth gal like you. Now, hide your eyes, dear lady. It'll all be over soon.

DEIRDRE: Hold me, Mr. Darrow. Hold me close!

A spark lit up the living room, as Mr. Lupino yanked the radio's cord from the wall. The dial went dark, and the fates of Trip and Deirdre faded from Lily's ear, leaving only the din of her bawling brother.

Mrs. Lupino dashed into the living room, shaking suds from her pruny hands, and scooped Alfie off the floor. Alfie's piggish little eyes peered over his mother's shoulder, and Lily could swear those eyes were smiling at her.

Her teeth clenched. Her nostrils flared. Her fists clawed into the carpet. . . .

"Bed!" snarled Mr. Lupino.

"But—" began Lily.

"No fuss!" said Mrs. Lupino. "Go and wash up for

bed." Lily grabbed her glasses, and stomped off down the hall. "And brush that hair!" Mrs. Lupino shouted after her. "You're looking ratty."

Lily stomped into the bathroom and slammed the door behind her. She grabbed a hairbrush from the cabinet, and started hacking at the stubborn knots of her long black hair. Past her scowling reflection, her eyes met the steely gaze of Trip Darrow, printed on the cover of a comic book sitting on the tank of the toilet. Trip stood, proud and heroic, with his fists on his hips, and Deirdre huddling beside him. Nobody made Trip brush his hair before bed. His hair was short and shiny, much more sensible for piloting rockets and battling the hordes of Planet Reptillia.

Lily propped Trip on the sink next to the mirror, opened the medicine cabinet, and swapped the brush for a pair of scissors. *Shwip-shwip. Shwip-shwip . . .*

Angry knuckles rapped on the door.

"Just a second!" Lily answered—*shwip-shwip, shwip-shwip*—as locks of black hair gathered on the tiles around her feet.

"You better not be reading comic books in there," warned Mr. Lupino.

"I'm not."

The doorknob rattled. "Lily Lupino, you unlock this door! Now!"

"I'm almost done! Geez," said Lily, dropping the last fistful of hair into the wastebasket.

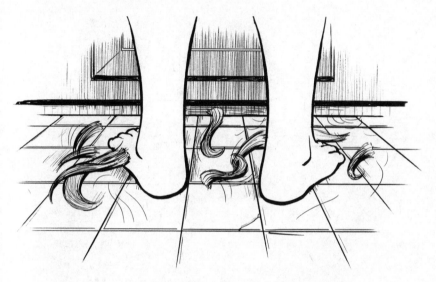

"Five . . . ," Mr. Lupino began. "Four . . . Three . . . Two . . ." Lily didn't care to find out what would happen when he got to "one." She unlocked the door, gave it a gentle push . . .

Once, when Lily was very little, she stuck a thermometer into a bubbling pot of pea soup, just to see if it would blow up. It did. Glass sprinkles flew everywhere, and Lily wasn't allowed in the kitchen for a whole year.

Tonight, when the door opened, and Mr. Lupino saw his daughter's handiwork, his face turned so red that Lily thought he might suffer the same fate as that old thermometer.

CHAPTER 2

Interrogation

The evidence lay neatly on the desk: a pair of scissors, three locks of wavy black hair, and one full-color issue of *Trip Darrow: Star Pilot*. Smoke curled from Mr. Lupino's pipe, glowing in the light of the desk lamp. He ran his fingers over his mustache, and scowled across his desk at Lily, who sat, staring into her lap.

Mrs. Lupino stood off to the side, steadying herself against the coatrack, with mascara streaking down her cheeks. She stifled her sobs, and her face brightened for a second. . . .

"We'll get her a wig!"

"No," sighed Mr. Lupino. "Anything convincing is going to be too expensive."

"Then we'll just have to keep her indoors, out of sight, until it grows back."

"And have her falling behind in school? No." He snapped his fingers. "I know! We'll say it was an accident: She wandered a little too close to your electric fan, and it ripped the hair right off her head!" He was clearly proud of this suggestion, and confused when it only made Mrs. Lupino sob all the more. He scowled at Lily. "Well, I hope you're proud of yourself! You've finally done it. You've broken your mother. And after all she's done to make a decent, normal little lady out of you. First you tear up your brother's favorite pig . . . I've never seen him so upset."

"I didn't tear it up. He did!"

"No tantrums!"

Tantrums! Little Alfie could be screeching like a barn owl, oozing from every hole in his purple face, and Mr. Lupino would say he was "upset." But if Lily so much as raised an eyebrow, it was always "a tantrum."

"Then you hole yourself up in the bathroom and . . . and . . . *mutilate* yourself! Whatever possessed you to do that to your head?"

Lily shrugged. She knew he wouldn't like her answer.

"You answer me right now, young lady!"

"Astronauts don't have long hair," Lily stated. "In zero gravity it floats around inside your helmet and tickles your face."

Mr. Lupino's face turned so red that his teeth and the whites of his eyes seemed to glow. Then he cooled himself with a long pull on his pipe.

"Tell me," he said. "Do you know any other girls your age caught up in this space baloney?"

Lily stared at her lap. She hardly knew any girls her age *period*, and had neither a clue nor a care what "caught them up."

"Of course you don't! Because they're all busy doing the things normal little girls do. What about that expensive tea set Nonna Lucille bought you? Have you ever even tried it?"

Lily shook her head.

"Well, soon you'll have plenty of time for tea parties,

because tonight you bid farewell to Mr. Trip Darrow." He tore the cover off the comic book. "And Flash Gordon, and Buck Rogers, and all the other space cadets." He ripped out page after page, until the comic was stripped bare. Then he tore the pages up, until there was nothing left but a mound of motley, star-spangled confetti. He brushed it off his desk, into the wastebasket. Finally he dumped the dregs from his coffee mug on top of them.

"Lily Lupino," he declared, "you're not an astronaut, so just put that thought out of your head for good."

"Why?"

"Because that's no job for a lady."

CHAPTER 3

The Purge

Lily sat on her bed, refusing to cry, while Mr. Lupino combed the children's bedroom for all traces of outer space and piled them into a cardboard box. He plucked the solar system mobile down from the ceiling. He stripped clippings of comics off the wall. Finally, with a sweep of his arm, he cleared the shelf over Lily's bed, catching squads of tin spacemen and windup robots in the box. Then he taped the box shut, and hoisted it out of the room. (He left the expensive tea set from Nonna Lucille in the corner, untouched.)

Mrs. Lupino carried the sleeping Alfie into the room, straddling her hip and drooling on her shoulder. She lay the boy in his crib, placed the one-legged Colonel Shanks beside him, kissed the boy's forehead, and headed for the door.

"Mom?" said Lily. Mrs. Lupino paused in the doorway. Lily wanted nothing but for her mother to look at her, but Mrs. Lupino just switched off the light, and closed the door behind her.

Lily tiptoed across the room, and leaned over her brother's crib. Even in his sleep, his piggish eyes looked like wicked little smiles.

"Bed!" roared Mr. Lupino through the wall.

Lily flopped onto her bed, and soaked her pillow with hot tears. Streetlights spilled into the bedroom through gauzy curtains, onto bare walls and empty shelves. She tried closing her eyes, but Mr. Lupino's scowling, reddening face was always there, waiting behind her eyelids.

So it was that Lily was still wide awake, charged with anger from head to toe, when Kosmo Kidd struck the Lupinos' apartment like a meteor.

CHAPTER 4

Stars in the Living Room

Lily sat up, as the last aftershocks rippled through the apartment. In his crib, Alfie gave a little squeak, then sighed himself back to sleep.

Lily slid out of bed, blew the dust off one of Nonna's teacups, set the rim against the bedroom door, and pressed her ear to the bottom of the cup. . . .

Aside from the syncopated snores of Mr. and Mrs. Lupino, the hall was silent. How had no one else heard the crash? No matter—it was up to Lily Lupino to investigate.

She put on her glasses, reached under her mattress, and pulled out the one item she had managed to hide from Mr. Lupino's ransacking wrath: the red, retractable Trip Darrow telescope she had cut out and taped together from the Sugar-Roos cereal box. She hung its string around her neck. A bit of extra string hung down, which she tied to the handle of Nonna's teacup. She figured it might come in handy.

She peeked out of her bedroom door. . . .

The hall was empty. Her parents' door was open just a

crack. She stalked past it into the living room.

The wood floor felt cold against her feet, and she could see her breath. There was a breeze from above. She looked up, and where there had been ceiling, now she saw *stars*. The night sky was spilling into her living room through a great big hole.

There was a smoldering trail scratched into the floor. Lily followed it into the kitchen. There, nestled in the misty glow of the open refrigerator, lay a small, rusty rocket ship, like something that had broken loose from a carnival ride. The living room rug was rumpled, pinched between the fridge and the rocket's dented grille. On the side of the rocket, a hatch was open.

Lily tiptoed between scattered leftovers, spilled condiments, and the shards of a broken jelly jar. She knocked on the rocket's rusty hull, and was startled nearly off her feet by an electronic chirp—*SQUIZZ&#$@!*—from the unmanned dashboard. But where was the pilot?

"Not a peep, lad!" hissed a high voice into Lily's ear. The voice echoed slightly, like someone talking into a tin can. A small, gloved hand grabbed her arm from the darkness, and something cold poked her back. "Do exactly as I say, and you won't end up deep-fried."

Deep-fried? Oh! It was a ray gun. Of course!

"Where are we?" asked the voice.

"Brooklyn."

"Planet Brooklyn . . . ?"

"No, Planet Earth."

"Ah, Earth: prison planet, maximum security. Right on course, then! This is a rescue mission. I'm here for Agent Argos."

"Who?"

"And we'll be leaving in a hurry, so be a good lad and keep your eye out for any Earth Men while I prep our getaway." He spoke like a London street-tough from a Sherlock Holmes mystery. His voice was high, but it had gravel in it.

"Could you please stop calling me 'lad'?"

"Eh?"

"I'm not a lad. I'm a girl."

The captor's grip loosened. Lily slipped free, and got her first good look at him. She couldn't tell how old he was. He looked younger than her, definitely smaller, but there was a seriousness in his eyes that was almost scary. He wore a black, red, and gold uniform that seemed cobbled together from attic scraps and box-top mail-in prizes, with a blue star stitched to the tummy of his tunic, and a slouching red garrison cap. And to top it off, he wore a big, fishbowl space helmet that made his voice sound tinny. He kept the ray gun pointed at Lily. His eyes narrowed to little slits in his brown face, and he sneered, showing a top row of tiny teeth.

"What's your game, boy-o?" spat the boy. "Wearin' a lady's dress!"

"I'm not a boy-o, either. I'm a girl."

"With hair like that?" The boy crowed with laughter, rocking so far back that his helmet fell off. Trying to act like it was on purpose, he sniffed the air.

"Air seems breathable," he said, and rolled his helmet back toward the rocket.

Lily giggled.

"Oy!" he barked. "The jig is up, lad. Off with the disguise!" He tugged at her nightgown. She slapped his cheek. The little astronaut dropped his weapon, and backed into the shadows to hide his moistening eyeballs, and nurse his stricken cheek.

"Oh, come on!" said Lily. "I barely hit you. Trust me, if I hit you for real you'll know it!" She picked up his weapon. "Here, you dropped your—"

"Give it here!" He snatched it. "Dangerous, that." It didn't look all that dangerous. In fact, it looked kind of cute, carved out of wood, with a fin on its back and a barrel that looked just like the honey dipper in Mrs. Lupino's junk drawer. The boy tucked it back into its holster.

"Sorry I smacked you," said Lily. "But you shouldn't go pointing guns at girls and trying to pull their dresses off."

"Aye," the boy answered gravely, staring a thousand-light-year stare. "War does things to a man."

Lily introduced herself, "Lily Lupino," and reached out to shake hands.

The boy didn't. Instead he placed his fists on his hips, and stuck out his chin.

"Kosmo Kidd," he said. For a moment, he reminded her a bit of Trip Darrow. He even seemed to grow a couple inches before her eyes. "Heard

21

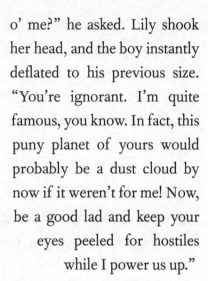

o' me?" he asked. Lily shook her head, and the boy instantly deflated to his previous size. "You're ignorant. I'm quite famous, you know. In fact, this puny planet of yours would probably be a dust cloud by now if it weren't for me! Now, be a good lad and keep your eyes peeled for hostiles while I power us up."

Gripping the rocket by the fin, Kosmo wrenched its nose out of the fridge, and dragged it to the middle of the kitchen floor. It slid easily on a puddle of Mrs. Lupino's chicken gravy. Lily saw letters painted on the side of the rocket, like on the bomber in the background of Mr. Lupino's framed WWII picture (except the rocket didn't have a lady with one leg pointing up, like on Mr. Lupino's plane). "*M-I-L-D-R-E-D* . . . ," she read. "Mildred? Your rocket's name is Mildred?" She tittered.

ZZOIP*&#@!!!—the rocket blurted angrily at Lily, startling her straight up into the air like the little squirrel at the shooting gallery.

"I mean, Mildred's a swell name," granted Lily. "Swell."

Kosmo tossed the helmet in through the hatch, and pulled out a huge winding key, as long as his arm. He inserted it into a socket in the hull and—*tic-tic-tic*—began to turn it.

"What are you doing?"

"Powering up the engine. What's it look like?"

"Oh. So, you came for who again?"

"Agent Argos. Finest field operative in space, til he got pinched by Lizard Lads in the Omaris Sector. Word is they shipped him here for safekeeping. So, what are you in for?"

"In for?"

"Aye, you're serving time here, aren't you? What for?"

"Oh. Um . . ." Lily tried to think of her worst crime. "I cut my hair."

"That your handiwork, is it?" Kosmo took a moment to admire Lily's short and shiny do.

"I call it the 'Trip Darrow.'"

"Oh, you know Trip? Fine spaceman. I taught him everything he knows."

"But you're a kid!"

Kosmo paused his winding to glare at her.

"No, lad, I'm *the* Kidd, always was, and never saw much use in being anything else. Now, have you seen Agent Argos or not?" He gave the key a final turn, and tossed it back into the hatch. "You may know him by his undercover name: Alfie."

Alfie? No, not *her* Alfie. The universe was a big place. *There must be lots of Alfies, right?*

"I know an Alfie, but all he does is dribble and stink."

"Aye, that's him! But don't let the disguise fool you. Old Argos is sharp as a shiv. Where they keeping him?"

"What are you gonna do with him when you find him?"

"Bust him outta jail, and rocket him back to HQ."

"Where's that?"

"Light-years away," he said. *Alfie, light-years away?* That sounded just fine to Lily.

"The 'brig' is this way," she said, leading Kosmo into the hall.

CHAPTER 5

The Liberation of Agent Argos

Lily stopped just short of her parents' door. Snores and darkness wafted through the crack. "Shh!" Lily whispered. "Don't wake up Dad. He hates monkey business!"

"*Dad*, you say?" sneered Kosmo. "Never could abide their sort," he said, and spat on the floor, "*P-tooey!*"

"Me neither," said Lily. "P-tooey!"

Kosmo drew his ray gun, and with a wolfish gleam in his eyes, poked his foot into Mr. and Mrs. Lupino's bedroom. . . .

"Wait!" whispered Lily, holding him back.

Part of her was itching to see what would happen if he went in. She'd never seen a disintegration before. Sure, she'd heard plenty on the radio, but a real live demonstration? What would it look like? Would Mr. Lupino melt into jiggly jelly, or glow red and pop into a cloud of smoke? But then she thought of poor Mrs. Lupino, waking up in the morning to find out she was no longer married to a man, but to a pile of gray ashes.

"Whose side are you on, lad?"

"If you alert the guards, you'll never get Argos."

"Aye. Clever lad." Kosmo followed Lily down the hall, into her room.

Kosmo stalked toward Alfie's crib.

"Locked up like a bloody animal. Savages!" He shook his fist in the air. "Oy, Argos! It's me, Koz," he whispered, rapping on the bars. "Time for our daring escape!"

Alfie's round, groggy face appeared between the bars.

"You sure he's your guy?" asked Lily. "I mean, look at him!" Alfie blinked and dribbled.

"I told you, that's his cover. He's as sly as a fox." He urged the toddler, "Go on, old man, lay some slyness on the lad."

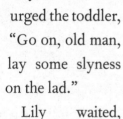

Lily waited, almost expecting to hear some strange new voice come out of her brother's mouth. . . . Until Alfie stuck his finger up his nose. Kosmo swatted Alfie's hand.

"Traumatized. Snap out of it, man!" Kosmo turned to Lily and asked, "Give us a hand here, will you?"

Together they hoisted the fleshy toddler out of his crib and set him on the floor, where he started whimpering.

"Here." Lily handed Alfie Colonel Shanks, and he quieted right down. "Or he'll cry the whole way. Trust me."

They stalked back down the hall to the rocket, wound and waiting in the kitchen.

"After you, old man." Kosmo tossed Colonel Shanks into the hatch, and Alfie clambered in after the pig. Kosmo sat in the pilot's seat, and saluted Lily.

"You're a good man in a pinch, lad. Sayonara!" he said, reaching for the hatch.

"Wait!" Lily exclaimed. "So . . . where you guys headed?"

"Back home. Fort Spacetronaut," Kosmo answered. The lads'll be wondering after us by now."

"What lads?"

"My crew, the Spacetronauts."

"In . . . outer space?"

"Outer space? Pff! *Outer* Outer Space!"

"What do you do there?"

"Oh, we do space missions, roughhouse, fight galactic villainy, race rockets. . . ."

"Explore planets?"

"All the time. Ta!" Kosmo was about to pull the hatch closed, when Lily caught it with her hand.

"You know," she said. "I'm training to be an astronaut when I grow up."

"Grow up? Why bother! All the best spacemen are kids—look at me!"

"You got room for one more?"

"What, up *there?*" Kosmo asked.

"Depends. Are you good at anything?"

"Lots. I can tell a red giant from a white dwarf, and I can always tell you which way is north. See?" She pointed her telescope through the hole in the ceiling, found the North Star, and pointed out the four directions. "Never Eat Soggy Waffles."

"Sure, brains are well and good, but can you fire a vaporizer pistol?"

"Sure," Lily assumed.

"Or fly a twin carbo-thruster space rocket—"

"Yeah," she guessed.

"—*through* a flaming meteor shower?"

"Probably."

"Can you wallop a moon troll?"

"I walloped you, didn't I?"

"Now see here, lad!" Kosmo fumed, jutting out his chin.

"I AM NOT A LAD!" Lily protested, stomping her foot. Why wouldn't it sink in? Maybe it was because of her—*Oh yeah!* "Hair!" she blurted. "I can cut hair."

Kosmo scratched his chin. "Now that you mention it, we don't have a barber on the crew. The lads and me could use the odd trim, eh, Mildred?" Mildred's answer was less than enthusiastic.

"Now, Mildred, don't be rude!" scolded Kosmo. "He can't help that, can he?"

"Is she talking about me?" asked Lily. Mildred chattered on.

Kosmo answered Mildred, "'Course he's up to it. You think I'd recruit him if he wasn't?" Mildred honked a warning. "Sure," said Kosmo, "I remember the last recruit, but—" Mildred interrupted. "Fine!" groaned Kosmo, raising his right hand and reciting after Mildred, "I, Kosmo Kidd . . . do swear to take full responsibility . . . for recruiting and training Lily something-or-other—"

"*Lupino*," Lily threw in.

". . . and not to get him disintegrated or shot into space like that last recruit, what's-his-name."

"Wait, who?"

Kosmo stuck out his hand, and shook Lily's.

"Congratulations, lad!

29

You're hired." Kosmo climbed out of the rocket. Lily was about to climb in, when Kosmo stared coldly into her eyes.

"Think hard on it, son. Space is no picnic: the most monstrous monsters, the vilest villains, black holes that'll turn you inside out, then squirt you out like toothpaste on the backside of the universe. Believe you me, space'll make a man out of you. You climb on board, there's no going back."

Lily nodded gravely, climbed in, and slid across to the passenger seat. Kosmo sat in the pilot's seat, and with a rusty squeak, pulled the hatch closed behind him.

CHAPTER 6

(Regular) Space

Mildred's insides smelled like leather and stale candy. From the outside, she had looked barely big enough for two, but the inside was surprisingly spacious. She had two seats up front, and room in the back for Alfie (who was already curled up with one velveteen hoof in his mouth), with extra room for at least two or three more Spacetronauts. Kosmo pounded the dashboard, and a panel of glowing gauges and bottle cap buttons blinked to life.

"Mildred, fire up scramjets and set trajectory. Ten . . . Nine . . . Eight . . ." Lily's seat grew hot and began to shake. Through the windshield, she saw that they were pointed straight at the open refrigerator.

"Um . . . ," she said, "don't we need a runway or something?"

"Nah," answered Kosmo, gripping the joystick. "We'll just aim for that bulkhead."

"That's not a bulkhead, that's the fridge!" Her seat was shaking so hard she sounded like Tarzan hollering on his vine.

"You may want to buckle that strap, rookie," urged Kosmo. "Five . . . Four . . ."

"What strap?" asked Lily, searching. "I don't see a—"

"Blast off!" cried Kosmo, slapping a big red button. The rocket shot forward, straight through the open refrigerator, and exploded out the other side in a spray of ketchup, mustard, and assorted produce. Lily's stomach jumped into her throat. City lights streaked past the windshield—up or down, she couldn't tell which—then suddenly fell away, leaving only the nighttime clouds sliding by, and beyond them, a sea of pinhole stars.

As the noise of the engine softened, Lily noticed Kosmo making noises with his mouth:

"Ffffrrrroooommmm . . . Vyarrrrnn! Shooooffff . . ."

"Why are you making that noise?" she asked.

"What noise? Vveeyooowwmmm . . ."

"*That* noise. With your mouth."

"That's not me, it's the engine. Sshhhhfff!" he said, misting the cabin with spit.

"Ew! You're spitting on me."

"No, no. That's condensation. Perfectly normal as you breach the atmosphere. Ffffshhhh!"

The full moon floated into view, so close that Lily could see every dimple in its silver surface.

"Ooo, look! The moon. It's so—"

"Mildred, lock on target . . . Fire! Tsew-tsew!" Kosmo pulled a trigger on the joystick, firing two bolts of golden light from Mildred's underbelly. In a hot white flash, the moon exploded, pelting the wind-shield with gravel.

"Um . . . You just blew up the moon."

"What, that asteroid?"

"That wasn't an asteroid. It was the moon. You just killed the moon."

"So? It was in my way."

Lily felt sad, thinking of how empty the night sky was going to look. But then she remembered that it wasn't *her* night sky, not anymore. In *Outer* Outer Space, there would be moons aplenty. She giggled at the thought of Mr. Lupino stumbling home from work on a newly moonless Brooklyn night, tripping over a planter and spilling his papers in the mud.

Through the porthole on the passenger side, the stars looked tiny and far away. Mildred must have been going very fast, but the stars weren't streaking by. They were just sitting there, still.

"Funny," Lily mused. "Outer space still looks far away, even when you're in it."

"Oh, this is still just *regular* Space. Outer Space is coming up shortly." And sure enough, they passed a floating road sign that read: NOW ENTERING OUTER SPACE.

CHAPTER 7

Outer Space

Not a whole lot happened during this phase of their journey, but Lily did make a few curious observations:

One) Outer Space did indeed feel much closer than Regular Space. Stars burned bigger and brighter, and whizzed by, so that Lily felt like the rocket was going much faster than before.

Two) Unlike Regular Space, in Outer Space you didn't need to know the constellations to spot them. Here their silver outlines were in plain view, and even moved around. This was good news to Lily, who had always felt bad for constellations, having to hold still for so long. In Outer Space, a ram could ram, Leo could roar, and Orion could loosen his belt once in a while (and did so, as they passed).

Three) Lily spotted two stars bobbing side by side, one large and red, the other small and white. She raised her telescope for a closer look, and saw that these weren't stars at all, but a lumbering red giant attempting to club an impish white dwarf, who teased the giant by skipping and giggling around the giant's trunklike legs.

Soon another floating road sign appeared, rougher than the last one, made of mismatched wood like something out of a covered wagon movie, with the hand-painted words, NEXT EXIT: *OUTER* OUTER SPACE.

CHAPTER 8

Welcome (?) to *Outer* Outer Space

Far ahead, through the windshield, Lily saw a golden glow, and felt a tickle in her tummy.

"There it is," announced Kosmo, "*Outer* Outer Space! Ready for the big leagues, rookie?"

The glow got bigger and brighter, and Lily could almost see the outlines of a faraway carnival.

But just as this starlit frontier wonderland was about to take shape, a wisp of red smoke slashed across the windshield, washing the vision away. Kosmo gasped, and jerked the hand brake. Mildred spun to a screeching stop, just short of a blood-red river of fog, blocking their way to the golden playground beyond.

"Slight detour, rookie."

"What is that?" asked Lily.

"The Murky Way Nebula. One big, creeping cloud of bad news, that. Gets a little bigger every time I see it. Steer well clear of there, rookie, and you'll do just fine."

He steered Mildred alongside the rambling fog, seeking a passage through, or over, or under the Murky Way, dodging its curling, seeping, seeking fingers.

"Keep your distance, Mildred," warned Kosmo. "If that fog catches a whiff, it'll be all over us like stink on a sock!"

"A whiff of what?" asked Lily.

"Juvenility, youth, kiddishness . . . Call it what you like, they don't take kindly to our sort in these parts."

"What's 'our sort'?"

"Kids."

Hulking shadows glided through the nebula, casting cold searchlights through the gloom. Mildred's engine began to sputter and pop, and she slowed to a lazy crawl.

"Fine time to wind down, Mildred!" grumbled Kosmo, and the rocket honked back, in a huff. "Oh well, keep an eye peeled for somewhere we can wind up."

He steered them into a field of craggy asteroids. "Too small . . . Too bumpy . . . Too holey . . . ," said Kosmo, seeking somewhere—anywhere—to land. At last, "Hallo!" he exclaimed, as a towering, three-eyed rooster in a mechanic's jumpsuit appeared, looming over one of the asteroids. Painted on a faded billboard with the words GLUCK'S GAS-'EM-UP, the rooster pointed a welcoming wing toward a rectangular opening carved into the asteroid.

"That oughta do," said Kosmo. They dipped under the sign, into the core of the rock, where they scraped to a halt on the stone floor, just as Mildred's engine ticked its last tick.

Kosmo grabbed the winding key from the backseat,

careful not to disturb the sleeping Alfie, popped the hatch, and slid out of the rocket. "Keep an eye out while I wind 'er up, will you?"

Lily poked her head out, and her blood instantly froze in her veins—looming over the rocket were three tall, broad, metal men. She rubbed her eyes and took another look—and saw that they were actually three fuel pumps, rusted over and draped in cobwebs. She slid out and joined Kosmo.

By Mildred's failing light, Kosmo was about to insert the winding key into the rocket, when—

BWAWKK!!! A squawk startled the key right out of Kosmo's hands. It clanged onto his foot.

"Yow!" he cried, hopping on the other foot, as a mangy rooster, in grease-stained coveralls, hobbled out from behind the fuel pumps, pointing a vaporizer rifle at Lily and Kosmo. He was bigger than an Earth rooster, and might have even stood a head or two taller than Lily, if he wasn't so stooped.

"It's Gluck!" Lily whispered, recognizing the rooster from the billboard, even though in person he looked much worse for wear, and far less friendly, with patches over two of his three eyes, and only a few stubborn feathers remaining in his leathery chicken hide.

"What do we have here?" Gluck clucked. "A coupla ankle-biters?" He said "here" like "heeyah," and "bit-ers" like "bitahs." He reminded Lily of the guy at the fish counter where Mrs. Lupino bought her salmon. Mrs. Lupino said he was from "Main," even though Lily never heard anyone on Main Street talk like a three-eyed space rooster. "Ankle-biters don't fare so well out this way, not since that mean ol' red fog rolled in. And folks caught harborin' ankle-biters don't fare much better. Besides, I'm clean outta rocket juice, so you may as well skedaddle."

"Just a quick windup, and we'll be outta your hair. Or, feathers," Kosmo said. "See, Mildred here runs on elbow grease."

"Mildred, you say? Mildred . . . ," mused Gluck. His good eye rolled back, as if looking for something inside his own skull. . . . "Well, I'll be plucked and peppered!" he exclaimed, lowering his weapon. "Do I have *the* Kosmo Kidd, Spacetronaut, right here in my very own Gas-'Em-Up?" He tilted his head back, and let out a crow that rang off the stone walls.

"Sh-sh! Keep a lid on it, fella!" whispered Kosmo.

"I trust you'll forgive an ol' bird being cautious in these unkindly times." He hobbled over to a wall covered in posters and flyers printed in red, white, and black ink. Lily could barely make out the words. She was an A-plus reader for her age, but the lighting in Gluck's was D-minus, and the print was small. Still, her eyes managed to pick out a few slogans, like:

At the top of every poster was the same emblem: a coiling black mustache.

Gluck ripped down a sheet of paper, and waved it at Kosmo. "Young man, could I trouble you for an autograph?" Kosmo took a yellow crayon out of a pouch on his belt, and scribbled on the paper.

"Can I see that?" asked Lily. He handed it to her. Between a printed picture of Kosmo's face, and the words "Kosmo Wuz Heer" written in yellow crayon, she read the printed words:

WANTED:

ONE

KOSMO KIDD,

SPACETRONAUT

THAT MOST JUVENILE OF JUVENILES, FOR THE CRIMES OF:

CAPITAL MISCHIEF, FIRST DEGREE MONKEYSHINES,

AND NUMEROUS COUNTS OF

HIGH-JINKERY

BY ORDER OF HIS MEANNESS, THE MEAN-MAN OF MORGO

Gluck lovingly folded the paper and tucked it into his breast pocket.

"Who's the Mean-Man of Morgo?" asked Lily, and that name was enough to sap the twinkle right out of Gluck's eye.

"Never mind about him," said Kosmo, but Gluck had already worked up the courage to answer, "The Scarlet Sourpuss, they call him. Menace of the Murky Way. Why, the Mean-Man of Morgo's about the evilest, drattedest, kid-snatchinest fiend that ever there was. He's got a face as red as the blood in your veins, and more meanness in that long, twisty black mustache o' his than all the other space villains in *Outer* Outer Space put together. Up there in his gloomy gray tower, scooping up all the stray kiddies he can get his evil red hands on!"

"What for?" asked Lily.

"Beats me, but it ain't for tiddlywinks!"

"That'll do, bird!" said Kosmo. "No need to go scaring the lad."

"I'm not scared," said Lily, but before she could even finish that short sentence, she found herself plenty scared. The blast of a foghorn shook the walls of the asteroid, so low that it was more felt than heard. Gluck's wattle shook, and his good eye glazed over with terror. Outside the entrance to the station, a tide of red fog rolled in, blotting out the stars and asteroids.

"The Murky Way!" Gluck squawked.

"Looks like it caught itself a whiff after all, rookie!" said Kosmo.

A cement wall, covered with snaking pipes and steaming vents, rolled by outside the entrance. Lily guessed it was the side of some impossibly huge, unpleasant spaceship. It jerked to a halt, spurting steam, and hovered there, rumbling from deep inside its mechanical guts.

"That'll be the Morgonites, out prowlin' for kiddos to haul back to their boss, ol' you-know-who. Batten down, little chickens, and I'll try to get rid of 'em. And if you've got any kiddish thoughts scampering about in them little heads o' yours, stomp 'em out pronto, or those Morgonites will smell it on you."

A gangplank clanged open, blasting cold light into the station. Lily and Kosmo crawled into Mildred. Kosmo sealed the hatch, and they balled up on the floor. Lily peered over the dashboard. Through the windshield, she saw two men in tall red helmets, with long gray faces, and long gray cloaks that hung all the way around their bodies. One carried a weird red space baton, with a trumpet shape at one end. The other had what looked like an extra-large—or, kid-size—butterfly net. They marched down the gangplank into the station, chanting in dreary unison:

44

Oobly-Eye, Oobly-Oo,
Find 'em, fetch 'em!
Rack 'em, stretch 'em!

45

Morgonites? Lily mouthed. Kosmo nodded.

Oobly-Eye, Oobly-Oo,
Seek 'em, find 'em!
Scoop and bind 'em!

Slithering alongside the Morgonites, a wisp of red fog branched off from the big fog outside, sniffing, seeking, zigzagging across the floor. The Morgonite with the weird baton loomed over Gluck.

"Decrepit yard-fowl!" he barked, in a low, bossy, bored tone. "We detect an air of *juvenility* on these premises."

"Juvenility?" said Gluck. "What, like young'uns and such? Why, we don't get much o' that up this way." Lily couldn't hear much of what the old rooster said, but it must have done the trick, because the two Morgonites turned back toward the gangplank. But then, from the back seat:

"Mommy!" cried Alfie, sitting upright, wide-eyed, chin quivering. Kosmo and Lily clapped all four of their hands over his yap, but it was too late. The Morgonites spun around. The red wisp darted straight at the windshield, and slid back and forth across the glass, sniffing. . . .

"Who occupies this derelict vehicle?" barked the net-carrying Morgonite, tapping Mildred's hull.

"Oh, there's nobody at all occupying it," clucked the rooster. "That's just some ol' junker I keep lyin' around for parts. Hasn't run in donkey's years!"

"Then explain the utterance."

"*Utterance*, you say? I'm sure I didn't hear any *utterance*."

"I distinctly heard this vehicle say, 'Mommy,' as in, 'I want my Mommy!' or 'Mommy! I crave sugar-rich fodder.'"

"Oh, well, I reckon I musta left the radio on, is all, last time I was tinkerin'." He jostled the rocket with his talon. "*Ahem*—I said, it must've been the *radio* you heard!" He gave the rocket another kick.

Lily muffled her mouth behind Nonna's teacup, and mimicked the sound of radio static: "Fsshhhh . . ." Then she spoke in a high, squeaky voice, like the kid from the Sugar-Roos commercial that always played during *Trip Darrow: Star Pilot*: "Gee whiz, Mommy! That sure is some big crunch!" Then, speaking as low as she could, she imitated the announcer: "Remember, kids! For that sweet crunch you crave, make it a *Sugar-Roos* morning! Fffshhh—"

Gluck silenced the rocket with another kick. "Funny, fussy contraptions, those ol' radios. Signal just comes and goes as it pleases!"

Lily heard a thump, as one of the Morgonites slapped something on Mildred's windshield. Then she heard their chanting voices fade back the way they came:

Finally she heard the rumble of the ship fading away.

Tap-tap. "All clear, kiddos," clucked Gluck. Lily peeked over the dashboard, through the windshield. Sure enough, where there had been red fog and gray cement blocking the passage, now there was a clear view of stars and asteroids.

Kosmo popped the hatch.

"Well, old bird," he said. "For a rooster, you're sure no chicken."

"Much obliged, Spacetronaut. Oh!" he exclaimed, handing Kosmo a slip of red paper from the windshield. "Morgonites left you a little something." Kosmo looked it over. . . .

"Bleeding parking ticket!" he sneered. He stuffed it in his mouth, chewed it, then spat the soggy wad at the wall. *SPLAT!* It hit the Mean-Man of Morgo—printed on a recruitment poster for Morgo Industries—right between his scowling eyes and stuck there.

CHAPTER 9

A Whisper of Whiskers

Mildred arced out of the Gas-'Em-Up, leaving a trail of sparks, and one cheerfully waving rooster, in her wake. . . .

Meanwhile, the soggy *SPLAT!* of Kosmo's spit wad had sent an invisible ripple through the vapors of the Murky Way. The echo traveled straight to the chilled heart of the nebula, to a curling precipice of red smoke, where a cement tower loomed. On the top floor, the *SPLAT!* echoed its way through an enormous circular window, into the secret laboratory of His Meanness, the Mean-Man of Morgo.

The lights were off. Techno-sorcerous gizmos and sharp tools glinted red in the nebula's glow. In their midst, slumped and slumbering in his high-backed chair, darker than the darkness all around him, sat His Meanness. His snore sounded like a rattlesnake on the loose, and with each breath, the two sides of his mustache coiled and uncoiled like lizard tongues.

At last the *SPLAT!*'s exhausted echo—dwindled to

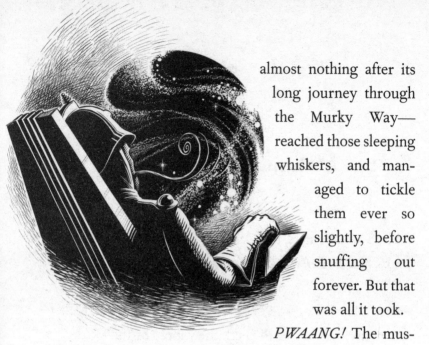

almost nothing after its long journey through the Murky Way—reached those sleeping whiskers, and managed to tickle them ever so slightly, before snuffing out forever. But that was all it took.

PWAANG! The mustache sprang to attention, spearing the darkness. . . .

Now, this might seem like a strange way for a mustache to behave, but not if you know a thing or two about Morgothronian anatomy. The whiskers on their faces work as antennae, tuned in to the vibrations of childish mischief, monkeyshines, and tomfoolery, which are the bane of every Morgothronian's existence. And in *Outer* Outer Space, there was one frequency more patently, potently juvenile than all the rest. . . .

The eyes of the Mean-Man jolted open. His hands groped blindly through a residue of nightmares, until he fully awoke to the meaning of his mustache's message: Wherever the little scamp had been, whatever he'd been up to lately in the far corners of the universe, Kosmo Kidd had come home.

MORGO

WE INTERRUPT THIS BOOK WITH AN URGENT MESSAGE FROM HIS MEANNESS, THE MEAN-MAN OF MORGO:

ATTENTION READER:

SINCE YOU HAVE REACHED PAGE 53 OF THIS INFANTILE DRIVEL INVOLVING WIND-UP ROCKETS AND TALKING CHICKENS, WITHOUT FEELING THE NEED TO DEPOSIT IT INTO THE GARBAGE, I MUST CONCLUDE THAT YOU ARE EITHER:

    A. A CHILD, OR

    B. A CHILDISH GROWN-UP

. . . NEITHER OF WHICH HAS ANY PLACE IN THE TOT-FREE GALAXY WE AT MORGO INDUSTRIES ARE BRINGING ABOUT.

I HEREBY ORDER YOU TO CLOSE THIS BOOK IMMEDIATELY AND CAST IT INTO THE NEAREST WASTE RECEPTACLE OR (PREFERABLY) FIRE*. FAILURE TO COMPLY MAY RESULT IN YOUR DETAINMENT AND REHABILITATION AT THE HANDS OF MORGO INDUSTRIES.

UNKINDEST REGARDS,

MMM

*MINORS: SEEK ADULT ASSISTANCE BEFORE INCINERATING THIS BOOK.

WARNING:

BY TURNING THE PREVIOUS PAGE, YOU ARE NOW IN DIRECT DISOBEDIENCE OF MY ORDERS.

BE ADVISED THAT IF YOU TURN ONE MORE PAGE, I WILL BE OBLIGED TO DISPATCH MY OFFICERS TO YOUR PRESENT LOCATION, WHEREUPON YOU WILL BE APPREHENDED AND DELIVERED INTO MY CUSTODY, TO BE DEALT WITH AT MY DISCRETION.

SO, DO NOT TURN ANOTHER PAGE!

(I REALLY, REALLY MEAN IT.)

SCOWLINGLY,
MMM

MORGO

VERY WELL, JUVENILE. YOU ASKED FOR IT.

READ ON AT YOUR PERIL!

PERTURBEDLY YOURS,
MMM

PSST! DOWN HEER. TERN TO PAJE 115 FER A TOP SECRIT MESEGE

CHAPTER 10

To Fort Spacetronaut

The barrier of red fog was finally starting to thin and pull apart, leaving an opening for Mildred to zip across, into the heart of downtown *Outer* Outer Space. A pack of hot rod rockets growled by, rattling Mildred's hull, and trailing black smoke. Mildred revved her engine, and roared straight to the head of the pack. They weaved between clacking billiard ball planets, skimmed tufts of cotton candy nebulae, and dodged the spinning, rocking rings of Planet Tilt-A-World.

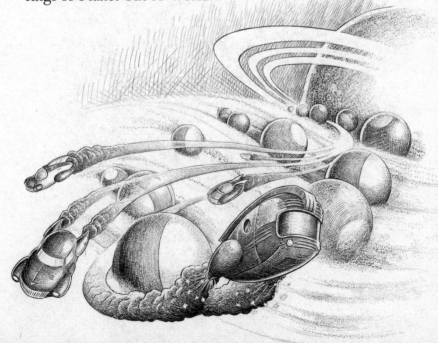

They sailed over a sparkling mountain range of rock candy asteroids, when Mildred split off from the others, and plunged into a dense forest of floating trees, whose gnarled roots dangled like old men's feet over the starry night. Branches whipped the windshield as Kosmo steered Mildred, pitching and yawing, through the thickening wilderness. Soon the trees were clustered so close that Lily could no longer see any stars between them. At last they reached the shining, golden heart of the forest, cradled in the knobby arms of the tallest, twistiest tree: Fort Spacetronaut, a tree-borne tin space shack, with trash-can-lid satellite dishes, and wire hanger antennae.

"Mildred, set entry course," said Kosmo.

"Aye, Captain," chirped Mildred (but what Lily heard was more like *SPWOP-dibbit*). Kosmo throttled forward, and Mildred hurtled toward a small opening in the lower half of the tree house. She barreled through, clipping the edge in a spray of splinters, skidded along a bumpy deck, and slammed to a halt against the far wall of a small hangar.

Kosmo opened the hatch and slid out of the rocket. Lily followed, coughing on the dust stirred up by their landing.

"Welcome home, old man!" Kosmo hoisted Alfie, still clutching Colonel Shanks, out of the rocket. "Whew! What's that smell?"

"That's Agent Argos. I hope you have diapers in Fort Spacetronaut," she said.

Kosmo placed Alfie at the base of a fire pole. "Right, old man. Up you go!" *Zhoop!* The toddler slid *up* the pole, through a hole in the ceiling. Kosmo was about to follow, but stopped, and looked at Lily in her nightgown, with the faded blue flower pattern, and frilly trim around the shoulders.

"Hang on, son," he said. "Make yourself presentable." From a rack on the wall, he handed her a pair of silver, space-age overalls.

"What's wrong with what I have on?"

"Spacetronaut Rule Number One." Kosmo pointed to a message, slapped on the wall next to the fire pole in drippy white paint:

MANE COMAND DEK:

LADS OWNLY
NO WIMMEN ALOWD!

"What? How come?"

"'Cause females bring nothing but trouble, that's how come."

"Well, too bad, 'cause I am one!"

"Right, lad. Time to drop the charade!"

"It's not a charade. I am a—"

"Sh-sh!" Kosmo leaned close and whispered. "See here, lad! All that 'I'm a lady' talk might pass muster back on Planet Earth, but this is *Outer* Outer Space. Now, do you want to be a Spacetronaut, or don't you?"

"Yes, but—"

"Then make like a man, and slip on them Space Trousers." Kosmo grabbed the pole and—*Zhoop!*—up he slid.

Lily stared at the Space Trousers.

She put her left foot in. She put her right foot in. She pulled up the trousers, tucked in her nightgown, and looped the straps over her shoulders.

She checked her reflection in Mildred's windshield. The trousers were baggy, and bunched in weird places. No matter how she shifted and twisted, the bulges never went away, they just popped up somewhere else. She got the feeling Mildred was looking at her.

"What!" said Lily.

But Mildred said nothing. Lily took hold of the pole, and—*Zhoop!*—up she went.

CHAPTER 11

The Spacetronauts

Lily slid up through a hole, onto a balcony overlooking the Main Command Deck of Fort Spacetronaut. "Looking sharp, rookie!" said Kosmo. "Welcome to Fort Spacetronaut. Not bad, eh?"

Not bad at all! The deck buzzed with the hijinks of rowdy young spacemen. There must have been at least a dozen boys, from the very small, to the slightly less small. Some were just back from, or just heading out to, jaunts amongst the stars, in fishbowl space helmets.

Two more were out on the porch, having a shooting contest.

"Pull!" cried a Spacetronaut marksman with a vaporizer rifle. Another pulled a lever, launching a fleet of miniature flying saucers into the night sky. The marksman shot every one of them out of the air like clay pigeons.

Another bunch of Spacetronauts sat on the floor, playing an explosive game of Dyna-Marbles that left all their faces blackened, and filled the air with the aroma of gunpowder.

The costumes of the Spacetronauts covered the gamut from buckaroos to buccaneers, but each and every outfit had one thing in common: a cutout star stitched to the tummy.

"Only the real crackerjack space chaps wear the star of the Spacetronauts," Kosmo explained. Then he leaned out over the balcony and bellowed:

"Oy, Spacetronauts!" Every boy in the fort dropped what he was doing, and performed the Spacetronaut Salute, an elaborate three-part routine ending with one finger blasting skyward like a rocket, while mouthing the *fffwoosh* of the engine.

"Behold, lads: Agent Argos, back from the dreaded prison planet Earth, all in one piece!" He stood Alfie on an apple crate, for all to see. "What do you say, old man? Any wise words for your old crew?"

The Spacetronauts waited, breathless. What new sights had he seen? What perils had he braved? What wisdom had he found in the far reaches of space?

Alfie opened his mouth. The Spacetronauts leaned in. . . .

But they got no wise words from Agent Argos's mouth that day, only a strand of drool that rolled off his chin and stretched all the way to the deck. Lily covered her mouth to hide her smile, or maybe to keep the words "I told you so" from slipping out.

Kosmo stammered, "He's . . . uh . . . had a bit of a trauma, see. Maybe it's best we just give him some room to recover." The toddler climbed down from the balcony, and the Spacetronauts parted, holding their noses, as Alfie tottered toward the nearest shiny object.

"But!" shouted Kosmo, with a triumphant clap. "I couldn't have done it without our newest recruit, Lily Something!"

"Lupino," Lily said, and performed the Spacetronaut salute—*fffwoosh*—nailing it on her first try.

"He's an Earth Man, but let's not hold that against

him. He's right clever, good in a pinch, and a fine barber. See there?" He pointed at Lily's head. "It's called the 'Trip Darrow.'" The Spacetronauts murmured and nodded. "Play your marbles right, he might just give *you* a trim!"

Lily saw two boys in the corner, scowling in her direction, whispering things that, from the looks of it, weren't too friendly. One was a tall, freckly boy in a coonskin cap, red cowboy boots, fringed gloves, and a rhinestone-encrusted space onesie. The other boy wore a chef's toque, and had a mustache that looked like it was smeared on with shoe polish.

"Right, lads!" shouted Kosmo, hopping down onto the main deck. "Space villainy ain't gonna battle itself, is it? Back to work!"

CHAPTER 12

Space Math

The Spacetronauts formed two facing ranks. Kosmo marched between them, the freckly boy in the coonskin cap marched beside him, and Lily shuffled after them, tripping over her baggy trousers.

Kosmo whispered to the freckly boy, "Anybody sit in my chair while I was away?"

"Don't you fret none, Koz," the boy answered. "I kept 'er cool for ya!"

Kosmo climbed into a raised bucket chair, so high that his little feet dangled a foot above the floor. On the wall behind him, painted in huge white letters, were the words MISHUN CONTROLL CENTR. The boy in the coonskin cap stood between Lily and the chair, and folded his fringed arms across his chest.

"Lily, meet Davy C. Rocket, King of the Final Frontier," said Kosmo.

"*And* best bosom friend to Kosmo

Kidd," Davy added, looking down his nose at Lily.

Kosmo took a piece of crinkled cardboard out of his belt pouch, and passed it to Davy.

Davy uncrinkled it and read aloud, "'Rescue Argos from Planet Earth.'" He climbed onto the shoulders of the boy in the chef's toque, to draw a line through the words chalked high on the wall, RESKEW ARGOS FRUM PLANNIT URTH. Then he crumpled the card, and tossed it into a bin marked MISHINS O'COMPLISHED.

"Well, fellers," Davy shouted, "Another Mission O'Complished!" The Spacetronauts clapped and hooted.

The wall was covered in chalk-written "missions" with lines through them. Many had souvenirs displayed beside them. (Since Spacetronauts were not A-plus spellers, Lily had to sound out the words in her head.) Next to the words GIV MAD MYESTRO 4TSEEMO A TAISTA HIZONE MEDISIN! (i.e. "Give Mad Maestro Fortizzimo a Taste of His Own Medicine"), she saw a pair of white, fifty-fingered gloves. On a shelf next to PILFER THE PEEPRS OF DOKTER OKULUS (i.e. "Pilfer the Peepers of Doctor Oculus"), there sat a jar of alien eyeballs, with pupils that looked around the room, in a single, unified gaze. And beside STELE THE TAEL OF LOTHAN LORDUV LIZZERDS (i.e. "Steal the Tail of Lothan Lord of Lizards") was a scaly, blue lizard tail, pinned to the wall, alive and twitching.

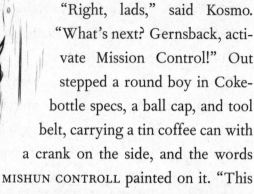

"Right, lads," said Kosmo. "What's next? Gernsback, activate Mission Control!" Out stepped a round boy in Coke-bottle specs, a ball cap, and tool belt, carrying a tin coffee can with a crank on the side, and the words MISHUN CONTROLL painted on it. "This here's Gernsback, the gadgetician, the nuts and the bolts of our operation."

Looking into Gernsback's blinking, magnified eyes, Lily got the weird feeling there was something there that shouldn't be, or maybe something *not* there that *should* be.

"Delighted. To make your. Acquaintance. Lily Lupino," said Gernsback, in a voice that was somehow mechanical and chipper at the same time. He stuck out a grease-blackened hand, and shook Lily's.

How come he talks like that? thought Lily. Then she wondered if she had accidentally said it out loud, because Kosmo said, "Gernsy, show the rookie how come you talk like that." Gernsback took off his cap. There was a scar across his brow, and Lily could see through his crew cut a row of bolts around the crown of his head.

"He scooped his brain out," Kosmo explained, "and stuck in an adding machine. Now he's the cleverest lad in space. Watch! Hey, Gernsy, what's the minus of . . . um . . . seven and two?"

"Seven. Minus two. Equals . . ." Gernsback's eyes rolled back, and inside the boy's head, Lily heard a whirring, clicking sound. "Five." The Spacetronauts all nodded, impressed.

"But that's easy!" said Lily. Right away she wished she hadn't, because every Spacetronaut whipped around to stare at her.

"Well, well, fellers," said Davy. "Looks like we got us a smarty-pants! Okeydokey, tenderfoot, if yer so smart, let's see who can answer first, you or Gernsy!" The Spacetronauts circled round for a scrimmage. "What's seven hundred plus . . . four *thousand*?"

The Spacetronauts gasped. Davy had gone straight for the big numbers! Gernsback bit his lip. His eyes rolled back. His brain whirred. . . .

But he had barely begun to calculate, when Lily said, "Four thousand seven hundred." Davy puffed up his chest.

"All right, then. Y'all try this 'un on fer size! What's . . . a cat . . . plus . . ." Davy scratched under his coonskin,

71

cooking up a real humdinger. He smiled like a coyote, and a breeze blew in from nowhere to tickle his fringe. "...a coat hanger?"

Gernsback's brain set right to work. Lily's stopped dead in its tracks. This was Space Math, not one of her stronger subjects. But she took a deep breath, closed her eyes . . .

The answer popped into her head, just as Gernsback was about to open his mouth. Lily shouted: "A sloth!"

Gernsback blinked at her, in shock, then took off his hat to Lily.

"Tell me. Lily Lupino. Are all. Earth Men. Clever. Like you?" The Spacetronauts cheered—all but Davy.

"Lucky guess, greenhorn," he sneered, then stalked into the corner to lick his wounded pride.

"Well, rookie," said Kosmo. "Care to earn yourself a Spacetronaut Star?"

"How do I do that?"

"You gotta 'complish a mission."

Gernsback held up the Mission Control can. Lily gave it a good crank, and out popped a card: NAB THE MENEMANS MOSTASH FRUMUNDR HIS VAIRY NOS.

"Well, rookie, what's it say?" asked Kosmo, kicking his giddy feet in the air.

Lily sounded it out aloud, "'Nab the Mean-Man's Mustache from Under His Very Nose.'" *The Mean-Man!*

Remembering the warning of Gluck back at his station, she shivered, and all of Fort Spacetronaut shivered with her.

"Nah, nah," said Kosmo, hopping down from his chair. "Let's save that mission for another day, shall we?" He snatched the card from Lily.

"What in heckfire for?" protested Davy, snatching the card back from Kosmo. "Ain't it about time we stuck it to that miserable red-faced so-and-so?" The Spacetronauts cheered at this. One stood on another's shoulders, and chalked the mission onto the wall.

"Draw again, rookie!" said Kosmo.

"Now, hang on a tick," argued Davy. "Are mine ears a'fibbin' at me, or do I hear the great and fearless Kosmo Kidd duckin' the will o' the Mission Control dingus?" He took Kosmo aside and whispered, "What gives, Koz? Y'ain't gone yella on me, have ya?"

"Yella? Ha!" Kosmo laughed. "Kosmo Kidd knows no fear, as you well know, Davy C. Rocket." He climbed back into his chair, and crossed his arms. "I just figured, this being the rookie's first mission, we ought to *ease him in*. There's plenty of other space bullies we can battle."

But Lily Lupino wasn't about to be *eased in*. She grabbed the card from Davy. "I'm not scared of some old Mean-Man of Morgo," she insisted, hoping it was true.

"*¡Oye!*" cried the boy in the chef's toque. "Not afraid of *El Diablo del Espacio*? *¡Que valiente chico!* This Earth

73

rookie has some guts in him, eh, *amigos? Soy* Pando, the chef." He took off his toque, and bowed like the bull-fighter on one of Mrs. Lupino's paperbacks. "*Bienvenido a nuestra casa en las estrellas.* Let's measure this *chico* for his Spacetronaut Star right away!"

"Now hold your horses, hombre," interrupted Davy. "He ain't even—"

But Pando held none of his horses, slapping Lily on the back, while Gernsback rifled through his tool belt for a measuring tape.

"Sir. If I. May," said Gernsback. Wrapping the tape around Lily's waist, he snagged the buckle on the Space Trousers. The straps came loose, and the trousers hit the floor. . . .

If there were crickets in space, you would have heard one now. Every eye in the place—even the ones in Dr. Oculus's jar—fell upon Lily.

CHAPTER 13

The Lads vs. Lily Lupino

The Spacetronauts crowded around Lily in her night-gown, with the fallen Space Trousers bunched at her bare feet.

"Boy! What in star-nation are you doin' in a dress?" Davy asked.

"It's a nightgown," said Lily.

Only Pando came to her defense. "Amigos, this frilli-ness must be a ritual garment of Lily's people, the robe of some manly Earth Man ritual."

"I dunno . . . Somethin's been sticking in my craw about this new feller," said Davy. "Scan 'im, Gernsy!"

Gernsback leaned in and covered one eye. The other eye rolled over and over in its socket, like a slot machine.

"Genus . . . HUMAN. Origin . . . PLANET EARTH. Sex . . ." *Ding!* His eyeball came to rest, and where there had been a pupil, now there was a pink symbol of Venus. "FEMALE!"

The word spread like wildfire among the panicking Spacetronauts.

"Uh-oh," said Kosmo to himself. He slid off his chair, and tiptoed out of sight.

"Code Pink!" cried Gernsback.

"Female on deck!" hollered Pando.

"Flank that filly, fellers!" cried Davy, and the Spacetronauts closed in around her.

"So I'm a female," said Lily. "So what!"

"Spacetronaut Rule Number One," sneered Pando.

"No. Women. Allowed," recited Gernsback.

"How come?!" said Lily.

"'Cause, missy, females just ain't fit fer space."

"Says who!"

"It's bio-logical. All flowered up and daintifed, gals make a man's head go funny, til next thing he knows, he's pickin' flowers instead o' fights."

"Oh, hogwash," said Lily.

"Koz, looks like you done been hornswaggled! This here *femmy-fatally* done bamboozled her way into our supersecret, man-only space base." He looked for Kosmo, but there was only his empty chair. "Koz?"

"There he is!" cried a squat Spacetronaut in a newsboy cap. Everyone turned to see Kosmo at the top of the fire pole, about to slide down into the hangar.

"Say, Koz, where you scurryin' off to in such a hurry?" asked Davy. "Sidle up here, and tell us just what you was thinkin' of, bringin' this here Earth Woman into our lads-only lair."

The Spacetronauts dragged Kosmo into the center of the deck, and stood him beside Lily.

"Spill it, Koz!" said Davy. "You gone frilly or somethin'?"

"Yeah!" taunted the boy in the newsboy cap. "Whatcha been doin' on Earth anyways, havin' tea parties?"

"Ha!" laughed Davy. "Another minute, this here vix-*een* mighta had us *all* pinkies-up and nibblin' tea cakes!"

"What's a tea cake?" asked Lily.

"Clap it, girlie!" shouted Davy. "Y'aint gonna feminize us with any o' yer lady talk. Well, Koz? Whatcha got to say fer yerself?"

Kosmo looked at Lily, then at the wall of Spacetronauts surrounding him, with folded arms and lowered brows.

"What can I say, lads?" said Kosmo. "This here she-spy got the jump on me."

"What?" cried Lily.

"Aye!" Kosmo continued. "Decked himself out like a lad, so I'd let my guard down. You know women, lads, all full of fibbery and falseness."

"I am not!" Lily protested, turning to the others. "I told him I was a girl, over and over and over. . . . I told him back on Earth, I told him downstairs. . . . He's the one who made me put on these dumb pants!" She kicked the Space Trousers. They flew through the air, and knocked the toque off Pando's head.

"Silence, spy!" hissed Kosmo.

"Silence, both o' y'all!" ordered Davy. "Now, Koz, this pains me somethin' awful, us bein' bosom mates and all. But here inside o' Fort Spacetronaut, if there's one crime wickeder'n *bein'* a woman, it's bein' a sucker to one. Ain't that so, fellers?"

All the Spacetronauts stared at the floor, murmuring their grudging agreement (except for Agent Argos, who was busy gnawing on Lothan's twitching tail).

"Well then, that about seals 'er. For the breakin' of our sacredest rule, Spacetronaut Rule Number One, I herely-by find both o' y'all . . . guilty."

"Guilty," echoed the mournful crowd.

"Hey, Gernsy," said Davy. "What's the sentence?"

"The sentence. Is . . ." Gernsback ticked through the filing cabinet in his head. "Spaceman's. Holiday."

"Spaceman's Holiday," chanted the crowd.

"Spaceman's Holiday?" shouted Kosmo. He turned to Lily and hissed, "Well done, rookie! Couldn't keep your pants on, could you!"

"Me?" Her nostrils flared. She turned to the others and asked, "So, what is a Spaceman's Holiday, anyway?"

But the crowd just repeated the words "Spaceman's Holiday," grinning like devils.

"Your molecules," answered Gernsback, "shall be de-sintegrated. Cast across the reaches. Of space. And instantaneously *re*-sintegrated."

"Where?" asked Lily.

Gernsback shrugged. "I haven't quite. Tackled. That part yet."

"Will it hurt?" asked Lily.

"No, no!" Gernsback assured her. "However. The procedure. Has been known. To tickle a bit."

"Come, lads!" pled Kosmo. "It's me, Kosmo Kidd, the original Spacetronaut! You really want to go de-sintegrating your own—"

"Now, Koz," said Davy, "your choices are two: Stand the gaff like a man, or whinny and whine in a most yella and unmanly manner."

"Well, then, as I'm *not* yella, there's nothing else for

it. Charge up the Tele-Moleculizer, and fetch me my helmet. And one more for this . . . *woman*."

"I get a helmet?" asked Lily. Her own helmet? Maybe a Spaceman's Holiday wasn't so bad. Besides, she wasn't exactly hitting it off with these Spacetronauts, so why not try her luck with the holiday?

Davy and Pando lowered two shiny, fishbowl helmets onto Lily and Kosmo, then marched them onto a contraption marked TELLA-MOLEKULIZR, whirring and sparking, with blinking bulbs, a big twisty antenna, and lots of buttons and dials to keep Gernsback busy.

"Any last words?" asked Pando.

"Kosmo Kidd can go suck an egg," said Lily. The echo inside the helmet sounded just like on *Trip Darrow*!

"No!" said Kosmo. "Only Spacetronauts get last words. How about . . . hmm . . . 'Mark me, lads: You ain't seen the last of Kosmo Kidd.'"

The Spacetronauts nodded—as last words go, those were pretty good.

"Very well," said Gernsback. "De-moleculizing in ten . . . nine . . . eight . . ."

On the floor under Lily and Kosmo, a glowing, spinning spiral appeared. It gave off a hum that tickled Lily's feet. And when the tickle reached her sides, she doubled over with giggles.

"Three . . . two . . . ONE!" With a sigh of grief, Gernsback pulled a lever.

The walls of Fort Spacetronaut slurped in around Lily and Kosmo, followed by trees, then stars, then—*ssshhloop-POP!!!*—darkness.

CHAPTER 14

Marooned

Then, just as breathing in follows breathing out, the universe slurped inward again and—*ssshhloop-POP!!!*—Lily and Kosmo were floating in a sea of stars. Lily managed to get ahold of her giggles, as the last of her molecules tickled their way into place.

An icy cold crept under her skin.

She looked down: Under her dangling feet, there was no ground, just stars. She looked up: stars. To the right: past Kosmo (who looked just as lost as she felt), stars. To the left: stars. Behind her: She guessed there were probably more stars, but with nothing to push off of, she couldn't turn around to check.

Her eyes began to pick out other, closer shapes in the blackness between stars. There was a reef of scattered asteroids, coated with barnacles and crustaceans. She saw a wrecked spaceship, snapped in half, with all its spilled insides sitting perfectly still, frozen in time. And a strand of sea green vapor rippled through it all like an ocean wave.

"Blimey, the Deep End!" Kosmo shuddered. "Of all the places to re-sintegrate!"

"What's the Deep End?"

"The Great Uncharted. Outer-est edge of *Outer* Outer Space. Some first day you've had, rookie. First you turn my entire crew against me, then you get us both marooned in deep space. . . ."

"*You* fibbed on *me*! I told you I was a girl. It's not my fault you don't listen!"

"And it's not my fault you get your kicks running about with boy hair!"

"*Astronaut* hair!" she shouted.

"Oh, have it your way, love. I'm off!" He began kicking his legs and scooping with his arms.

"What are you doing?"

"It's always suppertime in the Deep End, and I'd rather not be on the menu."

"Suppertime for who?" Lily's eyes darted from asteroid to asteroid. In every crag and cranny, she saw shining eyes, blinking, staring. "Or what?"

"Whatever's bigger than you."

"Well, you're never gonna get anywhere like that." She was right. For all Kosmo's kicking and scooping, he just looked like a worm wriggling on a hook.

"Oh, mind your own hide!" he panted.

"Fine, I will." Lily extended her telescope and scanned the stars. "Aha!" she exclaimed.

"What?"

"Can I borrow your ray gun?"

"What for?"

"That star just winked at me."

"So you want to kill it?"

"No, I'm gonna send an SOS."

"To a star? They tend to stay put, love."

"If a star winks, there might be something moving in front of it. Like a spaceship. With your ray gun I can send a signal and get us picked up."

"Or gobbled up. What if it's a great spiny star eel, out for his next meal?"

"Well, if you'd rather just float around in space til you shrivel up like a raisin . . ."

"So it's picked up, gobbled up, or shriveled up, is it?" Kosmo gave up his wriggling, and slowly drew his ray gun. "I don't know . . . Handing a weapon to a known saboteur . . ."

Lily grabbed the ray gun, took aim, and began to fire long and short pulses of light at the winking star.

"What are you saying to them?"

"It's Morse code. 'SOS . . . Stranded . . . Deep End . . . Rescue . . . Please . . .'"

"Say 'marooned.' It sounds better," suggested Kosmo.

"'SOS . . . *Marooned* . . .' You're right, that is better."

"Unless you're from Morgo!" Kosmo quickly added. "And if you are, don't come any closer! Just turn yourself around. There's nobody here, least of all two stray kids. You're seeing things. So just head on back the way you came and get your eyes checked."

"Slow down!" Lily's trigger finger couldn't keep up with Kosmo's mouth. She lowered the pistol, and finally asked the question that had been eating at her ever since Gluck's station: "Why are you so scared of the Mean-Man of Morgo?"

"Oy, you calling me yellow?"

"No."

"Well-right I'm not!" Kosmo boasted, puffing his chest up. "I once fought off a horde of lizard lads with my own two fists! I flew a rocket down a star eel's throat, just to find out what he ate for lunch. Kosmo Kidd fears no man, not even the Mean-Man of Morgo." He paused, and his voice began to shake. "And *he* scares the bleeding daylights out of me!"

"But why?"

"Never mind!"

"I won't tell a soul. I swear."

"*Solemnly* swear?"

"Solemnly swear."

"Cross your eyes, stub your toes, stick a spindle up your nose?"

This sounded a bit like an Earth rhyme Lily knew. She guessed it added up to the same thing, and recited:

"Cross my eyes, stub my toes, stick a spindle up my nose."

"All right." Kosmo took a deep breath. "His Meanness,

that is, the Mean-Man of Morgo, he . . . Well, he . . ."

"He what?"

"He sp—" Something caught his eye before he could finish. "Rookie!" he whispered, pointing straight ahead. "I think you *did* kill that star after all."

Indeed, where Lily's winking star had been, now there was an empty spot between stars. Then the star next to it snuffed out too, and the one next to that, and so on. The blackness spread to form the outline of a fish, waving to and fro, swimming toward them.

"Blimey! Looks like something saw your signal, rookie!" said Kosmo. "And I reckon they don't speak Morse code. Open fire!"

But Lily did *not* open fire, at least not soon enough for Kosmo. He made a grab for the pistol, knocking it out of her hand, and sending it spinning out of reach.

The fishy shadow grew, until it was as big as two crosstown buses stacked one on top of the other. In the middle of it was a bright spot—no, *five* bright spots, like a row of glowing eyes, staring down its prey.

Kosmo started kicking and scooping again, more frantically than before. And even though Lily knew it made no sense, because there was no air to push off from, she found *her* legs and arms kicking and scooping too. So now there were *two* tiny worms wriggling on invisible hooks.

As the shadow barreled toward them, its five bulging eyes blazed red. A mouth yawned open like a drawbridge. Lily stared past its spiny underbite, into its gaping, dungeonlike throat. . . .

WHOOOMM!!—the enormous mouth slammed shut around them, snuffing out every last star in the night sky.

CHAPTER 15

Molly-cules at Midnight

The aroma of grilled space varmints, cooked over a coffee can stove, still lingered in Fort Spacetronaut. The lights were out, except for golden starlight streaming in through the windows. The Spacetronauts were spread out on the floor, picking their teeth, and patting their bulging tummies.

Davy C. Rocket strummed his guitar and sang an old-time space lullaby. . . .

Oh, show me a place
Where the red rockets race,
And the stars sparkle brightly all day . . .

They all were all in agreement: It had been a jolly, jubilant—and 100 percent guilt-free—spaceman's shindig, not one bit tarnished by thoughts of a recently banished comrade. Honest!

'Cause seldom you'll find
Such a space to unwind
As the place where the Spacetronauts play.

Well, all right . . . Truth be told, as much as they all pretended to the contrary, not one Spacetronaut was feeling a bit jolly inside. The empty High Command Chair loomed in the center of the room. Its big white letter *K* reflected the starlight, with a ghostly glow.

Davy struck a sour note—there was that weird hum again, throwing off his pitch! It had been buzzing in and out of his ears all evening.

"Hey, Gernsy!" he whispered. "Did you remember to switch off the Tele-Whatchamacallit?" But Gernsback was already fast asleep, with his eyes rolling over and over behind his fluttering lashes.

Home, home in the stars . . .

Davy finally managed to sing *himself* to sleep. But his slumber was haunted by visions of his best mate, floating for the rest of his days among the endless stars.

Odds are you've never heard a fort full of snoring Spacetronauts, so imagine a forest of trees all being sawed down at once. Now try to imagine, in the middle of that racket, the gentle pitter-patter of two tiny toddler feet, in feety pajamas. That ought to give you some idea of why not one single Spacetronaut woke up when Alfie began exploring the fort and playing with things a two-year-old probably shouldn't touch.

He stepped into a Spacetronaut onesie, with a big star stitched to the tummy. It was so big on him that the legs and sleeves dragged behind him. He put on a fishbowl space helmet, which kept slipping down nearly to his navel. Then the top-heavy toddler crawled onto Gernsback's workbench, where he made a puppet show starring Colonel Shanks and a fully charged plasma pistol.

A glowing, humming spiral on the floor caught his eye. He decided that seemed like a much more exciting venue for his puppet show, so he slid off the bench, and tottered toward the spiral. . . .

Ssshhloop-POP!!!

There was a flash of light, like the entire galaxy was getting its picture taken. Every Spacetronaut in the fort sat up, rubbed his eyes, and seeing nothing out of place, went right on snoozing.

CHAPTER 16

A Fine Kettle of Fish

A low, babbling, churning sound came up through the floor. It might have been soothing, if Lily wasn't busy wondering what it was going to feel like to be digested by a giant space piranha. Her helmet must have rolled off, because the smell of fish guts was making her eyes water. She felt her way around in the dark, through a bramble of giant bones, on a floor that felt awfully hard for a fish's insides. In fact, it felt more like metal.

"Oy!" came a whisper out of the dark. "You there, rookie?"

"Hard to say," she answered. "I can't see a thing."

"Do you reckon we're dead?"

"No, if we were dead, our noses wouldn't still work."

"Aye, mine's working overtime. *Phleughh!* Fancy me, *Outer* Outer Space's number one Spacetronaut, demoted to fish food!"

"Well, we better find a way outta here quick, or we're both gonna get demoted to number two."

There was a chorus of high giggles.

A blast of colorful light filled the space. Shielding her eyes, Lily saw, standing over her and Kosmo, five girls in shimmery party dresses, pointing harpoons at them. Lily guessed they were around her age (or would have been if they were human). They wore silver sashes from their left shoulders to their right hips, and matching silver gloves. Their blue-green hair was tied in bouncy ponytails, with sea grass. Their ears and eyelashes were shaped like fish fins, and their faces were even more shimmery than their dresses, with fine scales that you could see when the light hit them just right.

Lily felt like she had stumbled into a sock hop on board a haunted submarine. A breezy doo-wop record crackled through a cockle shell speaker. Pink and turquoise glow-in-the-dark jellyfish hung like chandeliers, between rows of fish ribs. On the rusty walls hung trophies of past catches: gaping, sharklike jawbones with silver teeth; a pickled, eighteen-tentacled Octodecopus in a jar; a pair of deadly Sycoraxian pulcher pincers . . .

There were two rows of glittery, vinyl-padded chairs bolted to the floor, facing a windshield made up of five big domes, or . . . eyes!—at least, that's what they had looked like from the outside.

A girl stepped to the front of the pack, wearing a pearl-encrusted tiara, and chomping a piece of pink bubblegum.

"Well, well, ladies, what do we got here? A coupla worms?" She pronounced "worms" like "woyms," like a girl from down Flatbush Avenue, not across the universe. She crouched over Lily and Kosmo. "Say, these worms is human! What are a coupla humans doin' out here in the Deep End?"

"Um . . . ," began Lily. "We're a wee bit off course."

The girls laughed.

"I'll say!" laughed the girl in the tiara. She leaned in for a closer look. "Wait a sec . . . This bespectacled human looks kinda female."

"I *am* female," said Lily.

"'Zat so? Well, how do you like that!" said the girl in the tiara, helping Lily to her feet. "What do they call you?"

"Lily Lupino of Earth."

"Earth? A jailbird, are you! I bet they make 'em pretty salty down there, huh?"

"I get by," said Lily.

"Yeah, stick around. We'll see about that. We're the Piranha Sisters. I'm Donna, skipper of this rig, and that's Juana, Lana, Shawna, and Shirl. We could use another pair o' fins around here. Interested?"

"I don't know. What do you guys do?" Lily asked.

"Oh, you know," said Juana. "Float around, mostly. Shoot the breeze, listen to records . . ."

"Yeah, till something real big comes along, that is," added Lana.

"Yeah," said Shawna, "then we hunt that sucker down and—"

POP! Donna popped a big pink bubble. ". . . take a big, juicy bite out of it!" She grinned, gnashing her gum, and for a second, Lily thought she saw sharp points at the ends of Donna's teeth. "So, Specs, you in?"

"Sorry, ladies," said Kosmo, climbing to his feet. "But we really oughta be—"

"Sure, why not!" said Lily. Kosmo gaped at her.

The sisters cheered. Shirl handed Lily a silver sash. "That's Altairian Mirror Shark skin, Specs," said Shirl. "Deadliest fish in the Deep End."

"Second deadliest!" shouted Shawna, boastfully.

"You never see 'em coming, just your own reflection," said Shirl. "And then it's too late. That big ol' mouth opens wide and *WHAMMO*! You're fish food."

"Sharp, ain't it?" asked Donna. It sure was! It was the shiniest thing Lily had ever laid eyes on. She slipped the sash over her left shoulder, and across her right hip.

"Welcome aboard, Specs!" said Donna.

"Rookie?" whispered Kosmo.

"Oh yeah!" said Donna. "I almost forgot about boy-worm here. He looks kinda familiar, doesn't he? What do they call you, boy-worm?"

"They call me Kidd. *Kosmo* Kidd."

"Ha! Sure," quipped Shawna. "And I'm Davy C. Rocket. My marmot-top's at the cleaners!" The whole crew laughed, except for Shirl. She walked over to a locker on the wall, and opened it. The inside was decorated with *Outer* Outer Space memorabilia (including a fair amount dedicated to the Spacetronauts). She peeled down a wanted poster, handed it to Donna, and whispered in her ear.

"Hot dog!" Donna squealed, flapping her ear-fins. "It really *is* Kosmo Kidd! Gee whiz, what a catch."

"Ladies," said Kosmo, tipping his cap, "always nice to meet a few fans!"

"So, sailor," Shawna cooed, "what's a galaxy-hopping *gallant* like yourself doing out in these lonesome shoals, anyway?"

"Yeah, don't that beat all!" squeaked Juana, shoving Shawna aside. "*Outer* Outer Space's primo bachelor, right here. Why, I could just go belly up!"

"Fins off, ladies!" ordered Donna, and they scattered like a school of fish. "The Spacetronaut is spoken for. Now step aside so I can *pin* this here paramour."

"P-p-pin me?!"

"You heard me! You and me, we're gonna be steadies." Shirl tossed Donna a clamshell brooch. Donna unhooked the pin on the back.

"Steadies? Sorry, love. Not looking to settle down, me. In fact, the rookie and me were just leaving. Right, rookie?"

But Lily didn't hear him. She was busy noticing how her new mirror sash changed color depending on where she stood.

"Aw, how cute!" said Donna. "Little spaceman thinks he's got a choice. Ladies, shall we educate him on how things work out here in the Deep End?"

"*You catch it, you keep it,*" recited Juana.

"*You catch it, you keep it,*" echoed the others.

"Lana, play something romantic while I do the honors," Donna ordered.

Lana switched the record. Syrupy strings crackled from the cockle. Donna backed Kosmo flat against the wall.

"Rookie!" Kosmo called out.

But Lily didn't hear him. She was busy admiring the control panel of the ship. It had a sonar screen, a mother-of-pearl dashboard . . . And what was that joystick made of? Some kind of carved bone?

"Oh, come on," said Donna. "This ol' bucket could really use a man's touch."

"Yeah," said Shirl. "This deck could use a good swabbing."

"And these dresses ain't gonna press themselves," added Juana.

"How are you in the kitchen?" asked Lana. "You better shuck those prawns good."

"And don't forget the eyes," added Shawna. "Ooo, I can't stand those beady little eyes!"

"And if it gets cold," said Donna, leaning in so close that Kosmo felt the breeze of her batting eyelashes, "maybe you and me can even *hold fins*."

Kosmo tried to make a dash for it.

"Hold him, ladies!" Donna commanded. "This worm's got some wiggle in him." The crew held him steady, as Donna brought the brooch close.

"LILY LUPINO!" cried Kosmo.

It was the first time Lily heard her full name from Kosmo's mouth. She turned, just as Donna was about to puncture the breast of Kosmo's tunic.

"Let go of that Spacetronaut!" said Lily.

The needle scratched across the record. (Why? No one bumped it. But it suited the moment, so nobody looked into it.) Everyone looked at Lily, who suddenly felt a little timid.

"So, uh," she said. "Maybe it's time for the boy-worm and me to, you know, hit the road."

"What gives, Specs?" asked Donna. "Are you a Piranha Sister, or ain't ya?"

Lily took off the mirror sash, folded it neatly, and laid it on the dashboard.

"I see," said Donna. "But I'm still skipper around here, see? And I'll pin who I wanna."

"Pin yourself. He said no, didn't he?"

"So?" said Donna. "What are you gonna do about it, fish bait?"

"Come over here and find out," said Lily, hoping she sounded tougher than she felt.

"Oooo!" said the sisters.

"Why should I?" asked Donna.

The only answer Lily could think of was that she'd heard it on *Trip Darrow*, like the time the chieftain of the Ice Lords threatened to marry Deirdre against her will, so Trip challenged him to a wrestling match for her hand. Or when the captain of the Laser Pirates of Praxxa tried to make Deirdre his bride, so Trip challenged him to a shooting contest for her hand. Or when the Rat King of Rodentia was going to marry Deirdre, unless Trip could beat him in a footrace (which wasn't really fair, pitting

Trip's two feet against the Rat King's four, but Trip won anyway). Such contests of valor happened so often in space, Lily figured it must be some kind of rule.

"You really expect me, Donna Piranha, skipper of the Piranha Sisters, to scrap with some wormy fleck of flotsam?"

"*Expect* you to?" said Lily. "No, I *dare* you to."

Donna blew a giant pink bubble. . . .

CHAPTER 17

Duel in the Deep End

POP! Donna's bubblegum burst, and she gnashed it in her teeth. "All right, Specs. You want a taste? You got it!"

The Piranha Sisters cheered, and flapped their ear-fins. It had been a long time since their last duel. They just needed to decide what form this duel would take.

"Dorsal sparring!" shouted Lana.

"Bah, kid stuff!" sneered Shawna. "How about a good gill-grappling match?" The sisters kept shouting out ideas, but each one had to be ruled out, because Lily didn't have the right anatomy.

Finally Lily managed to entice them all with an ancient mode of Earth combat that hadn't yet found its way to this corner of space. . . .

After Lily had explained the rules, a space was cleared, the spectators circled round, and the two combatants took their places, face-to-face. They decided Juana should preside over the match.

"All right, ladies," said Juana, "you both know the

rules. The count is three, protect yourselves at all times, and let's keep it clean. Now, bring 'em together. . . ."

Lily reached out her hand.

Donna took off her glove and clasped Lily's hand, leaving both of their thumbs free and upright. Donna's thumb looked almost human, except for the fine scales, and a shiny blue-green thumbnail. Her thumb certainly had the height advantage, but she was going to need it, against Lily's strength and experience.

"*Four, three, two, one . . . ,*" recited Juana, "*I declare this war begun!*"

Both thumbs held still, waiting for the other to make the first move. . . .

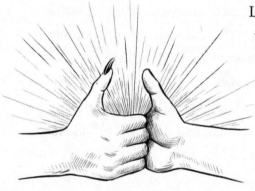 Lily broke the stillness with a small nod of the distal phalange, and soon both thumbs were dipping and curling around each other, like two cobras daring each other to strike.

Lily swept low, grazing Donna's thumb across the proximal phalange. Donna took the bait, slamming her thumb down toward Lily's.

But this was just the move Lily was counting on. She

ducked to the left, whipped back around, and pinned Donna just above the knuckle.

"One!" counted Juana, as Donna writhed to free herself. "Two!"

But Lily's move was as clumsy as it was fast, and the full force of her grip wasn't centered. The slickness of Donna's fine scaly thumb didn't help either. Donna's thumb slipped free just before the count of three, and retreated, crushed but not beaten.

Then Donna's thumb lunged, so quick and furious that it caught Lily off guard. It hooked Lily's thumb, tackling it into the crook of her own folded index finger. Lily yanked and jerked, but couldn't escape the force of Donna's grip. Donna smiled with the corner of her mouth, and this time Lily was sure she saw sharp points at the ends of her teeth.

"One!" called Juana.

Lily bent at the middle knuckle, and pressed the tip of her thumb hard against her own hand. This gave her just enough leverage to shift the angle of Donna's grip. . . .

"Two!"

Lily's thumb rolled clear, and Donna's thumb snapped down with full force. And before it could get up again, Lily's thumb had already swirled back around, and hammered back down upon Donna's, clamping it squarely below the middle knuckle.

"One!" called Juana. "Two!"

Try as Donna did to free herself, she and Lily both knew the count was a pure technicality.

"Three!"

Lily and Donna let go of each other's hand. Donna stared in awe at her throbbing, defeated thumb.

Lily looked at Kosmo. Was that admiration she saw in his eyes? Or gratitude, even? Or was it just plain relief, for the bachelorhood that was nearly stolen by a fish maiden of the deep?

"What can I say?" said the skipper. "When you're licked, you're licked. You want this Spacetronaut, Specs? He's all yours." She raised Lily's hand in the air, and the sisters applauded.

"You're one salty dog, Specs. You sure you can't stick around?"

"No, I got too much space to see," said Lily.

"Suit yourself." She tossed Lily the mirror sash. "Here, keep it. We'll save you a seat."

Lily put on the sash.

"Shirl, set a course for Gorgon's Wharf," said Donna. "We'll drop these two off, and maybe even squeeze in a little shore leave, whadda ya say?"

The whole crew cheered.

But before Shirl could punch the coordinates into the dashboard—*POING!! POING!!*—a red blip appeared on the sonar screen, big and rectangular, with a fin on its back.

"Belay that!" Donna slid into her seat at the front, and took the helm. "Strap in, gang!" The sisters strapped themselves into their seats, and Lily and Kosmo strapped into the back row.

"What is that?" asked Lily.

"Beats me!" cried Donna. "I've never seen such a whopper!" Her pupils widened, black and shiny, until there weren't any whites left in her eyes. Her mouth

spread into a hungry smile, showing off her needle-sharp teeth. The rest of the crew squealed in delight, flapping their ears and bouncing in their seats. Their eyes all went black, and they bared their fangs.

Their prey appeared in the windshield, a far-off spark zipping between the coral asteroids. Donna throttled forward, and the spark grew closer. Lily saw the afterburners of an enormous gray spaceship, like a floating cinderblock with a fin on its back. She had seen a glimpse of something just like it, back at Gluck's station. And from the terror in Kosmo's eyes, she knew Kosmo saw it too.

"Turn back!" Lily shouted. "That's no fish!" But her voice was lost in the scream of the engine.

The sea green vapors and coral asteroids fell away, as the ship sailed right out of the Deep End into bare, open space. That was enough to scare even the Piranha Sisters, fangs and all, except for Donna, driving them onward after their prey.

A blood-red fog rose in the windshield, and the gray ship dived straight down into it.

If Lily didn't warn Donna, the skipper was going to steer them all straight into the clutches of Morgo. Lily had hollered herself hoarse, but the engine drowned her out. So she had no choice but to climb to the front seat and shake some sense into the skipper. She unbuckled her belt, but at that very moment, Donna throttled forward, sending the ship into a nosedive, and sending Lily into a backward somersault, through a swarm of weightless fish bones, and thudding against the back wall of the ship.

Kosmo unfastened his seat belt, and tumbled after Lily. They found their space helmets bobbing in midair among the bones, put them on, and began scrambling for an exit. Any exit.

Lily spotted a circular hatch in the floor, with a big red button next to it, and some alien writing. She shrugged. Kosmo shrugged. Red fog filled the windshield. Lily slapped the button.

The hatch opened like an iris. The vacuum of space reached in, groping around for anything that wasn't strapped in or bolted down. It grabbed Lily and Kosmo by their ankles, and yanked them out into the gusting red fog.

They slid along the piranha ship's rusty underbelly,

barely dodged the blazing afterburners and the swaying steel tail fin. . . .

Well, *one* of them did, anyway. Kosmo wasn't so lucky. The tail fin swatted him on the backside, and sent him spinning like a top, out of the nebula.

The red fog swallowed Lily, cutting her off from the stars, and from Kosmo. Scarlet clouds wound around her, and would have surely hissed and howled like dragons, if they had the lungs for it.

Then her helmet rattled with a familiar, impossibly low foghorn, and a chorus of foghorns brayed in answer. From every direction, giant gray rectangular forms peeked out of the fog, and cast their cold searchlights through the vapor. Just when Lily was sure she had been spotted, there was a flare of flame deeper in the nebula. It was the Piranha Sisters' ship, flaring its afterburners as it rocketed ahead after its prey. The gray ships all banked, and thundered off after Donna, Lana, Shawna, Juana, and Shirl.

Lily caught herself, for just a second, feeling more than a little relieved. She felt ashamed of the feeling, but before she could properly scold herself, one of the gray ships pulled to a stop, swung its searchlight around, and captured Lily in its cold gaze.

"Rats." Lily groaned, as the ship turned and thundered toward her.

CHAPTER 18

Comet Hoppin'

"Rats." Kosmo groaned, bobbing over the Murky Way, watching helplessly as the Morgo Space Trawler caught Lily in its Capture Beam, slurped her up, and roared off, leaving a curling red wake in the fog. And it was easy to guess where it was headed: straight to the heart of the Murky Way, to the Tower of Morgo, a place Kosmo Kidd had done a fine job of finding excuses *not* to visit for quite some time. As the Trawler's afterburners shrank to a twinkle, Kosmo was gripped by an unfamiliar sensation: loneliness.

He tried whistling a few bars of a new Kosmo Kidd theme song he was working on, but the echo inside his helmet only made him feel more alone. If ever Kosmo Kidd, Spacetronaut, came near to facing the truth of his own helplessness, this would have been that moment—*would have been*, if it were not for a passing comet, summoning a very useful memory into his brain. . . .

COMET HOPPIN':
A Handy How-To
by Davy C. Rocket

Welcome, pard'ner, to the age-old art o' comet hoppin', a handy and happifyin' mode of cosmic conveyance. Heed these three easy steps, and you'll be ridin' the Star Tail Express faster'n you can say "fuzzy buzzard britches."

1. First and foremost is gittin' its attention. Comets bein' a most prideful bunch, it's as simple as flingin' a few choice barbs in its direction. Hit below the belt if ya gotta. And if all else fails, remember: Nothin' riles up a comet like disparagin' its dear ma.

2. Just as soon as you see it pivot and start a-chargin' at ya, hunker down, hoist one hand skyward, like as if to pluck an apple off a lofty limb.

3. Just when that comet's fixin' to plow on through ya like a toro in Toledo, feint right, and grip it by the tail. Not too high, mind, or your hand'll burn up redder'n a cad's keester on paddlin' day!

Kosmo giggled. Davy was always good for a laugh, like the time he said Pando's ambrosia salad tasted like it came out of a goose that had eaten some marshmallows and fruit. This was probably because Davy was steamed that Pando had put grapes in the ambrosia salad; Davy—it is well-known—does not care for grapes in his ambrosia salad!

And this reminded Kosmo of the time Pando stuck grape chewing gum in Gernsback's brain, making Gernsback talk with a stutter for two weeks.

And by the time Kosmo remembered that this probably wasn't the best time to be remembering things, the comet had nearly passed him by.

So, just as Davy instructed, Kosmo shouted out the first insult that popped into his head:

"Oy! Sparkle-Pants!"

The comet took no notice.

"I'm talking to you, Twinkle-Toes!"

But still the comet stayed its course.

"What's the matter, Shiny, your mother forget to . . . um . . ." Kosmo couldn't think of how to end this barb.

But it didn't matter, because the mere mention of the comet's mother had done the trick. It skidded to a sparking halt, reared to face Kosmo, and charged.

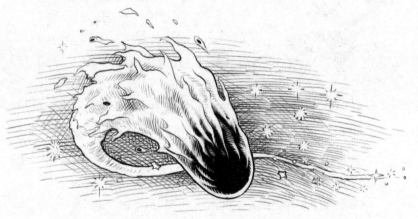

Kosmo raised his hand high above him. As the comet got closer, it suddenly occurred to Kosmo that he didn't know where in *Outer* Outer Space he wanted the comet to take him, once he caught it.

Planet Christmas is lovely this time of year, he thought.

But, ever the steadfast hero of the stars, he decided, he must brave the perils of Morgo, and go after Lily.

Or, thought Kosmo, *I could find a nice eatery somewhere. I could use a bite.*

But, ever the steadfast hero of the stars, he decided he must brave the perils of—

Or maybe stop by Gorgon's Wharf. A little R&R seems
in order.

BUT! Ever the steadfast hero of
the stars—

"Fine!" sulked Kosmo. "Bleedin' Morgo it is, then!"
His bones went cold at the thought, even as the flaming
comet barreled straight at his head. He feinted right, just
like Davy said to do. Then he reached into its blinding
light, groping for anything that might be a tail. . . .

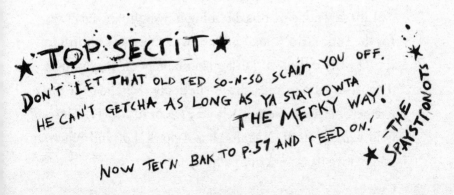

★ TOP SECRIT ★
DON'T LET THAT OLD RED SO-N-SO SCAIR YOU OFF.
HE CAN'T GETCHA AS LONG AS YA STAY OWTA
THE MERKY WAY!
NOW TERN BAK TO P. 57 AND REED ON!
★ —THE SPAYSTRONOTS

CHAPTER 19

To Morgo

Morgo Space Trawlers don't have windows. If they did, this is what the captive Lily would have seen as she neared her unhappy destination:

Countless Trawlers streamed like arteries into the cold core of the nebula, where the red vapors converged in a curling crimson precipice, like a petrified tidal wave. Perched atop the curl, the Tower of Morgo scanned the galaxy with a cold beam of light from its scowling penthouse window. And wherever that cruel gaze fell, in whatever merry corner of *Outer* Outer Space, a momentary chill would seize even the happiest heart.

Lily saw none of this, bobbing in weightless darkness for the entire trip. She didn't know if there was air inside the Trawler or not, so she kept her helmet on, just in case. Then, somebody must have suddenly switched on the gravity, because she fell with a *plop* onto the Trawler's cold cement floor. A gate blazed open, hot and white, and before her eyes could adjust . . .

Oobly-Eye, Oobly-Oo . . .

. . . a kid-size butterfly net swished over her, pinning her
arms to her sides.

Snare 'em, hook 'em!
Charge and book 'em!

Standing outside the Trawler were two Morgonites,
like the ones she'd hidden from back at Gluck's Gas-
'Em-Up. Here, now, in the cold light of Morgo, she got
her first good, clear look at the Morgonites: their tall red
helmets, their squeaky red gloves up to their elbows, the

billowing gray cloaks that wrapped around their whole bodies, and their long, gray, bored faces. One held the long handle attached to the net, and the other carried that same weird red baton as before, with a trumpet at one end.

"For the crime of juvenility in the first degree," said the one holding the net, "within the jurisdiction of His Meanness, the Mean-Man of Morgo, you shall forthwith be delivered to His Meanness for immediate and irre-versible Dejuvenation™."

"What does 'Dejuvenation™' mean?" asked Lily, always eager to add a new word to her vocabulary.

"Silence, vermin!" barked the other Morgonite. He aimed his baton at Lily, and pressed a button. The trum-pet let out a sound like a goose burping backward under-water, and she felt a thump against her tummy. A wave of pins and needles zinged through her whole body, her knees buckled, and she toppled over.

The Morgonite holding the net slid her out of the ship, and they dragged Lily through a bright hangar, past countless spaceships parked in neat rows. There were gargantuan Space Trawlers, flat-bottomed Scows, and squat little Star Skiffs, all made of cement, all look-ing like they had been carefully designed to take all the fun out of space travel.

They rounded a corner into a wide hallway, busy with Morgonites, all waddling with bored purpose. Through the gray cement sameness of it all, another kind of sameness struck Lily: *RED*. It wasn't that there was a lot of it—there wasn't. It was that there was absolutely *none* of any other color in Morgo. No blue jay blue, no Granny Smith green, no cerulean, no nothing but fire engine red to break up the endless gray.

Another pair of Morgonites marched past in the other

direction, dragging another netted kid along the floor.

"Hey!" called Lily.

"Silence, vermin!" shouted the Morgonites, and in seconds, the kid was out of sight.

The Morgonite pair dragged Lily into a massive lobby full of elevators. There must have been hundreds of them, with doors hissing open and shut, and Morgonites coming and going. They dragged her into one of them, and the doors hissed shut behind them.

One of the Morgonites tapped a control panel. A staticky screen popped up, projected in midair. A dour blue face appeared, scowling through cat-eye glasses.

"Madam," said the net-holding Morgonite. "Another specimen for His Meanness, found floating in the Murky Way." The eyes glanced down at Lily, and a reedy voice answered through a crackly speaker:

"Fine. Bring it on up."

DING! The elevator car rocketed upward, and Lily's heart sank into her stomach. Then with a jerk, it shot sideways, sending her sliding across the floor, and slamming into the wall. It changed direction several more times on its swift climb through the tower, and Lily slid and bumped like a hockey puck against the walls. Somehow, the Morgonites remained with their feet firmly planted.

CHAPTER 20

What "Dejuvination™" Means

DING! The car stopped so suddenly that Lily flew off the floor, and the net was the only thing that kept her from hitting the top. She landed with a thud. The Morgonites removed the net and lifted her onto her feet. Her legs wobbled as the last of the pins and needles drained out of her. The doors hissed open, the Morgonites shoved Lily out, and the doors hissed closed behind her.

She was in a long, narrow waiting area. On two long benches facing each other was a gathering of slouching, sneering, scuff-kneed, flipped-up-collar, juvenile space riff-raff. Back in Brooklyn, Earth, Lily had managed to go her whole life without getting sent to the principal's

office. Now, here she was, her first time in space, and she was already waiting on the bad boys' bench. At the far end was a big red door marked: DEJUVENATION™.

"What does Dejuvenation™ mean?" she asked, but the boys just stared at her.

"Get a load o' the guy in the dress!" hooted a boy in a striped T-shirt, chomping on a licorice cigar. This got a big laugh.

"I ain't a guy in a dress. I'm a girl with astronaut hair." This got an even bigger laugh.

"Astronaut, huh?" chided a boy with the shell of a popcorn kernel lodged in his buck teeth. "Where'd you get that goofy helmet, astronaut?" Helmet? Oh yeah! She had gotten so used to it, that she forgot she had it on.

"Fort Spacetronaut," Lily answered, taking it off. The boys grumbled, unconvinced.

"Can it, ya goons," said a slick ruffian with one black eye, a black bomber jacket, and a toothpick in his teeth. They all quieted right down. "Lemme see that, kid." Lily handed the ruffian the helmet, and he looked it over. "This here's the genuine article. Kid, you really been to Fort Spacetronaut? No foolin'?"

"Cross my eyes, stub my toes, stick a spindle up my nose," said Lily.

"Hot dawg!" cried the ruffian. "A full-fledged Spacetronaut! So, what'd they pinch you for?"

"Just bein' a kid, I guess. You?"

"Yeah, just bein' a kid too, I guess." Then he added, "Plus sayin' curses. And scrappin'. And stealin' chocolate bars. And hoppin' fences. And talkin' with my mouth full . . ." The list went on and on, until he either reached the end of his rap sheet, or got sick of talking about it. "Can I try 'er on?"

"Go ahead," said Lily.

The ruffian put on the helmet, and checked his reflection in Lily's mirror sash. "Radioactive! Get a load o' me, fellas, I'm a genuine Spacetronaut!" The boys laughed as the ruffian pretended to float around the room, making space breathing sounds. "It'll take a lot more than some Dejuvy-whatever to poop this party, dig?"

But in his spaced-out bliss, the ruffian missed the hiss of the Big Red Door and the squeak of high white boots striding in through a cloud of red smoke. Every smile in the room wilted, as the ruffian ran straight into a woman in a crisp gray uniform. She had ice-blue skin, cat-eye glasses, and silver hair pulled into a bun so tight that it seemed to be stretching her face across her skull.

"Who's the blue lady?" Lily whispered, recognizing her eyes from the screen in the elevator.

"Miss Meniscus," whispered one of the boys, shuddering. "Secretary to you-know-who."

With a white-gloved hand, Miss Meniscus swatted

the helmet off the Ruffian's head, and with the other she took him by the ear.

"Radioactive!" shouted the ruffian, as he was dragged into the curling smoke. The door hissed shut.

Lily and the other riff-raff waited for what might have been minutes, but felt like hours, wishing they could think of something to say to break that terrible quiet.

Finally the Big Red Door hissed open, and through a waft of smoke, out waddled a freshly minted Morgonite. To Lily's horror, she saw that he had one black eye, and a toothpick dangling from his lip. She looked for traces of the ruffian under that droopy scowl, but he was gone, along with the slightest blip of *radioactive*.

"Did it hurt?" Lily asked him, with a lump in her throat.

"Silence, vermin!" he barked.

Miss Meniscus strode into the room. "Now, who's next?" As she paced up and down the rows of seated scamps, even the stoutest of them shrank under her ice-cold gaze. "Which of you vermin shall receive His Meanness's attentions next? Are there any particularly rambunctious rascals among you today?"

She reached Lily, and leaned over her, glaring. Lily was glad the secretary was wearing those cat-eye glasses, because they seemed to be the only thing keeping those bulging eyeballs from rolling right out of their sockets and onto Lily's lap. "Ah!" said Miss Meniscus. "Here's a curious specimen, a boy in a dress!"

"I'm not a b—"

"Tch-ch!" Miss Meniscus pinched Lily's lips shut. "Boy, you will speak only when asked." She let go of Lily's lips.

"I said I'm not a—"

The secretary reached again for Lily's lips, but this time Lily dodged her grip, and bit down.

"Eeee-YOUCH!" shrieked Miss Meniscus, shaking her wounded thumb in the air, to the giggling delight of the boys on the bench. She took a deep breath, took a fresh look at Lily, and hissed, "Ahhh! You'll do just fine!" She grabbed Lily by the ear, the Black-Eyed Morgonite grabbed the other, and they hauled her through the smoke-filled doorway.

CHAPTER 21

His Meanness

Lily stepped through the red smoke, and on the other side of the Big Red Door, stepped into a room so vast that she wondered if it was a room at all and not the Murky Way itself. It was so lofty that it had its own sky indoors. And if there were walls, they were hiding behind curtains of red smoke that rose from vents in the cement floor. It reminded her of a temple or cathedral in some faraway land she had only seen in pictures. High on the far wall was a circular window—so big that her entire building back in Brooklyn would have fit through it easily—facing the swirling vortex of the Murky Way.

"Sire!" Miss Meniscus called across the room. "Another specimen."

Ahhhh, welcome, little ankle biter!

At first Lily thought the voice had come from inside her own head, maybe an echo of some forgotten nightmare. Then, the red smoke peeled back and Lily saw, below the big window, a high-backed chair facing a gray slab of a desk, covered in sharp, shiny tools with barbed

ends and glinting, keen edges, and teetering stacks of paper. The chair had its back to Lily, but she saw red fingers drumming on the arm of the chair. And sticking out of where a head ought to be, something black and snakelike was wriggling.

The red hand pointed to another chair in the middle of the room, bolted to the floor, the sort of unfriendly-looking chair you'd sit in to get a tooth pulled.

Have a seat.

Lily's feet obeyed, against her will, shuffling toward the chair. Hanging from a scaffolding, a huge, bulbous laser cannon was pointed right at the chair. The word DEJUVE-NATOR™ was stamped into the side. Smoke curled from its nozzle, which was still glowing red from its latest use.

Lily thought about making a run for it. If she was quick enough, she could slip straight past Miss Meniscus and the Black-Eyed Morgonite, and back through the Big Red Door. But how far would she get? Who cares! Sure, they'd catch her eventually, and drag her right back here. But so what? Better later than now! Go! Run!

Have a seat.

She sat.

Tell me, vermin, what manner of mischief has brought you before me today, hmmm?

And when that voice *hmmm*ed, it went high like a slide whistle. The high-backed chair turned to face her, and there he was: His Meanness himself, the Mean-Man of Morgo, in a gray uniform with a blocky letter *M* on the chest, and domed epaulets on the shoulders. His face was the color of hot, flowing blood, under the brim of his tall helmet. And there, curling out from his upper lip, was the most astonishing feat of facial follicles ever achieved in humanoid history, a serpentine black

mustache that writhed and danced with a life of its own.

She remembered how brave she felt back in Fort Spacetronaut, reading the words on the card:

NAB THE MENEMANS MOSTASH FRUMUNDR HIS VAIRY NOS.

But here, face-to-face with His Meanness, the idea that any Spacetronaut could ever muster the mettle to nab that mustache from under his very nose seemed like a ridiculous joke. Lily would have laughed, if she wasn't busy being scared out of her wits.

"Out infecting *Outer* Outer Space with your infantile tomfoolery, no doubt?" said His Meanness. He stood up, terrifyingly tall, and tied a white apron over his uniform. His mirror-black shoes clicked across the floor, as he walked toward Lily, sliding a pair of white gauntlets up to his elbows.

"What's the matter, little vermin?" asked the Mean-Man, while Miss Meniscus and the Black-Eyed Morgonite clamped Lily's wrists and ankles into the chair. "Catamarynth got your tongue?"

Lily thought back through all she had said and done since leaving Brooklyn, but couldn't think of anything she'd done wrong. In fact, she was pretty sure she had acted like a fine, upstanding space hero.

"I didn't do anything."

"Untrue, Your Meanness!" barked the Black-Eyed Morgonite. "He bit the Miss!"

"Lout! Was I speaking to you?" shouted the Mean-Man. "For that impertinence, you will now"—His Meanness gave it a moment's thought—"tie your insolent tongue in a knot."

"As you wish, sire," answered the Black-Eyed Morgonite, without hesitating. "Bowline?"

"Hmmm . . . Sheepshank."

"Very good, sire." The Black-Eyed Morgonite opened wide, stuck out his tongue, and grabbed it with both hands. . . .

Lily couldn't bear to look, but she couldn't avoid hearing a sound like stretching, squeaking rubber. And when she dared to look again, the Morgonite's tongue was sticking out of his mouth, tied in a sheepshank knot fit for a sailing vessel.

"It's true, Your Meanness," said Miss Meniscus. "The specimen did bite me." She removed her glove, and showed him her swollen thumb. "See?"

"Hmmm . . . Dental incisement of the manual extremities," said the Mean-Man. "Not a bad little specimen! Perhaps we ought to test out the new prototype, hmmm?"

"But sire, is it ready?" asked the secretary.

His Meanness shrugged. "Isn't that why they call it a test?"

"As you wish, Your Meanness." Miss Meniscus walked away, through the curtain of smoke, and the Black-Eyed Morgonite followed her.

Alone with his latest specimen, His Meanness took his first good look at Lily. "Zounds, boy!" he cried. "What are you doing in a dress?"

"I'm not a boy."

"Oh, what sort of creature are you then?"

"A girl."

"A girl in space! What's the matter? Take a wrong turn en route to the tea party, did we?"

"No, I'm an astronaut."

"A *girl* astronaut, are you? What a delicious imagination you have, young man." His Meanness leaned in close, and sniffed Lily. Then he drew back and gasped.

Miss Meniscus returned, wheeling out a steel cart, with a metal case the size of a cigar box.

"Your prototype, sire," she announced. The Black-Eyed Morgonite followed, rolling out a much larger cart, with a blinking apparatus the size of two refrigerators.

"Never mind," sighed His Meanness, as his whiskers drooped onto his chest. "It's a *girl*," he sneered.

"A girl? Human?" gasped Miss Meniscus. "In space?" She arched an eyebrow at Lily, a little curious, but mostly disgusted.

"And since I'm not in the business of Dejuvenating™ harmless little she-things," said the Mean-Man, "release the specimen."

"Very well, sire," said Miss Meniscus. "My apologies for wasting your time." She and the Black-Eyed Morgonite unclamped Lily's wrists and ankles.

His Meanness pulled a pad of pink papers from his pocket, scribbled something, tore off a slip, and handed it to Lily. "You're free to go. Take this to Level Six, Tele-Transit Depot, and they'll whisk you home to Mommy and Daddy in time for breakfast."

Lily was almost to the Big Red Door, when His Meanness called after her, "Oh! And little one, I do apologize for any unpleasantness. My Morgonites must have mistaken you for a *real* astronaut!"

Lily stopped. There was nothing on the other side of that Big Red Door but Brooklyn, Earth, and *Trip Darrow* lying torn-up and soggy in the trash. Over there, the only way to get to space was through a radio.

Lily stuffed the pink slip in her mouth, and crunched it in her teeth. She turned around, puffed up her cheeks, and marched straight toward His Meanness.

"Halt!" shouted the Black-Eyed Morgonite.

"Shoo, little lady," said Miss Meniscus. "Scoot!" But Lily pushed right past her.

Before either of them could shout a word of warning, Lily fired the soggy pink wad out of her puckered lips, nailing His Meanness squarely between the eyes.

The Mean-Man stood, still as stone. He blinked twice, dabbed the spittle from his forehead . . .

PWANG!!! His whiskers sprang out straight.

"Seize the girl!" he hissed. The Black-Eyed Morgonite grabbed Lily. "The vile thing!" raged the Mean-Man. "Perhaps a test run is in order after all. Charge the Actuator!"

"Charging the Actuator, sire!" Miss Meniscus flipped a switch on the huge apparatus. It coughed to life, rattling and humming, nearly shaking itself off the metal cart.

The Mean-Man reached into the metal case and took out a bulbous ray gun; a miniature, handheld version of the monstrosity hanging from the ceiling.

"Behold!" cried His Meanness. "The brand-new Deluxe Dejuvenator™, Sidearm Edition!

Compact, convenient, and portable." Miss Meniscus ran a cable from the huge apparatus and plugged it into the handle of the pistol. "Well, almost portable." He pushed a button and the pistol glowed, lighting up his face like a stoplight. "Why bother bringing the brat to justice, when you can bring justice to the brat? Soon, there won't be a single cranny of *Outer* Outer Space beyond my Dejuvenating™ reach!" He laughed a horrible, wheezing laugh. "Secure the specimen."

Miss Meniscus held Lily's left arm, the Black-Eyed Morgonite held her right, and they both leaned as far away from the target as they could.

"Little one," gloated His Meanness, "this will hurt a great deal. But don't worry! After it's over, you won't mind. In fact, you won't care about a thing! You'll finally be free of all those nasty urges and infantile frivolities, a full-grown and productive member of my staff, just like your tongue-tied friend here!"

The Black-Eyed Morgonite might have blushed at the compliment, if his face weren't permanently gray.

His Meanness closed one eye, took aim, and tensed his finger upon the trigger. . . .

As Lily stared down the glowing nozzle, do you think she regretted her crude and unladylike act? Does a zebra regret its stripes? In a matter of seconds, she would know nothing but *Oobly-Eye, Oobly-Oo*, and the occasional *Silence, Vermin!* But until then, she was Lily Lupino, Girl-Astronaut.

Outside the window, a shooting star pierced the red clouds of the Murky Way and rained golden glitter through the gloom. Was it *Outer* Outer Space's way of giving her a hero's send-off, one last glimpse of joy, before she forgot forever what joy was? She closed her eyes, and waited for the big *BZZERP!!!*

She waited . . .

And waited . . .

But there was no *BZZERP!!!*, only a dull crash that shook the floor under her feet.

When she opened her eyes, the Mean-Man had set down the Dejuvenator™ pistol, and was running his fingers up and down his twitching whiskers, as if trying to tune in a faint signal. . . .

"Sire?" asked Miss Meniscus.

The Mean-Man tapped a button on his helmet. A tiny

microphone slid out, and an antenna poked out of the top.

"Yes, hi. Security? I— . . . Hold?! No, I will *not* hold! I'm the Mean-Man of Morgo. I hold for no— . . . Is there someone else there I can speak with? . . . All right, hand him the receiver while you go and scour your impudent mouth with floor soap . . . Yes, hi. Mean-Man of Morgo here. I have reason to believe we have a breach, an intruder in our midst. A certain Spacetronaut. Put all sectors on red alert, and inform me the moment you've— . . . Wait, say that again? Small, bothersome fellow? Star on his tummy? Hold him there! I'll be down in—oh—ninety, ninety-five seconds."

He switched off his helmet-radio and bounded off through the Big Red Door, clicking his heels together and crowing, "Hoo-hoo!"

"Your Meanness!" Miss Meniscus called, running after him. The Black-Eyed Morgonite waddled after her. "No!" she shouted. "Stand right there, and guard that little one." She sprinted out the Big Red Door, after her master.

CHAPTER 22

A Perfectly Good Speech Wasted

The trip in his private Osmosis Tube, from the top-floor Dejuvenation™ Lab, all the way down to the Juvy Pound at the very bottom of the tower, gave the Mean-Man a chance to think up a good speech to mark the occasion. When the pod reached its destination, he gave his cells a moment to recongeal, then he stepped out into the dim corridor. He had to bend over, because the Juvy Pound's ceiling was just high enough for its juvenile prisoners.

Miss Meniscus came sprinting around the corner, from the elevator bay down the hall. (Her trip from the lab had taken longer than his; conventional humanoid elevators move at a snail's pace compared to a state-of-the-art Morgothronian Osmosis Tube.) She bent and followed her master into the Juvy Pound, panting, "Your Meanness! May I ask what—"

"I have him, Vivian!"

"Him *whom*, sire?"

"Him *him*! Here, in my grasp! The loathsome varmint has finally crash-landed right in my lap!"

"*Him* him? Can you be sure?"

"These whiskers never lie, Vivian."

A stooped Morgonite jailer welcomed them.

"Sire, your Spacetronaut awaits," he said, leading them past rows of child-size cells to a waist-high door at the end of the tunnel. Miss Meniscus lagged behind. She had learned to keep a safe distance, especially when His Meanness's emotions were running hot.

The Mean-Man paced outside the cell, savoring the moment.

"So . . . ," he began, "here you are at last, Spacetronaut. I was beginning to think that latest chastening I gave you, back on Planet Moltar, had scared you off for good. Yet here you are, bless you, shivering like a trapped rat, as the curtain draws back for the final act of our galactic pas de deux! Now, Kosmo Kidd, look on me, ye naughty, and despair. For at long last I shall teach you the meaning of the word . . . OBEY!"

He flung open the cell door. . . .

Tak-tak-tak-tak-tak. Miss Meniscus heard clashing cymbals echoing inside the cell, and a high-pitched giggle. The Mean-Man reeled back, pinching his nose.

"Your Meanness?" asked Miss Meniscus. "What's—"

"Cretin!" hissed the Mean-Man at the cowering jailer.

"I'm sorry, Your Meanness," said the jailer. (Apologizing to the Mean-Man was purely a reflex among Morgonites, who never really cared enough to be sorry about anything.) "So very, very, very—"

"Yes, you should be, raising my hopes like that! Just for that, I want you to . . ." He tapped his chin, dreaming up a punishment. "Paddle your fanny."

"As you command, sire."

"Hard! If I catch you sitting without difficulty, I shall be upset." His Meanness marched back down the hall, and settled back into his Osmosis Tube.

"Sire?" called Miss Meniscus, but her master had

140

already sealed the hatch, crossed his arms over his chest, and let his cells scatter into the jet of vapors, carrying him back toward the Dejuvenation™ Lab.

Miss Meniscus approached the cell, peered through the open door. . . .

The stink of a long-soiled diaper slapped her in her blue face. There, giggling on the floor of the cell, was *not* Kosmo Kidd, but Alfie Lupino, still wrapped in the oversize Spacetronaut onesie with the star on the tummy, and clutching Colonel Shanks.

Now, as surprising as this was to His Meanness and company, it really shouldn't come as any surprise to you, who have been reading this book. Because you, no doubt, remember how down and distracted the Space-tronauts were, after sending their beloved Kosmo on his Spaceman's Holiday—so down and distracted that none of them bothered to reset the Tele-Moleculizer. Therefore, when little Alfie toddled onto the machine, it de-sintegrated and re-sintegrated his molly-cules smack in the middle of the Deep End, just as it had Lily's and Kosmo's. In no time, the two-year-old was swallowed by a spiny star eel, which was promptly caught by a Syturnian space poacher. Knowing of the Mean-Man's taste for Deep End delicacies, the poacher swiftly delivered the creature, on ice, and for a hefty fee, to the Tower of Morgo. There, His Meanness's personal chef cut open the Star Eel's belly, and out spilled one small, pudgy, recently re-sintegrated toddler.

Alfie's chin quivered at the sight of Miss Meniscus. "Mommy?"

The secretary shivered in disgust, hissed at the foul creature, slammed the cell door, and ran back down the corridor—but not before reminding the jailer, "Get paddling!"

Alone in the Juvy Pound, the jailer started looking for something he could use to carry out his punishment.

CHAPTER 23

A Lousy First Day

Stand right there and guard that little one.

Those were the Miss's orders, and by golly, the Black-Eyed Morgonite wasn't about to foul up his first day on the job any more than he already had. So he kept his Magno-Baton raised, with the trumpet side aimed at the little vermin in the dress and glasses, who was sitting cross-legged in the middle of the floor.

Something metal clattered in the corner. He turned, squinted . . . Was that a boy-shaped shadow, flitting through the curtain of red smoke? Before his eyes could focus, it was gone.

When he looked back at the vermin in the dress and glasses, its face looked weird, different. The corners of its mouth were spreading up and to the sides, as if pulled by invisible hooks. What did it mean? He had a feeling he used to know. He scowled and grimaced, trying to think. . . .

"You okay, big fella?" said the vermin in the dress and glasses.

The words *SILENCE VERMIN!* rose in the Black-Eyed Morgonite's throat, but all that came out of his mouth was:

"Ayeh, euhih!" (It's tough saying consonants with your tongue tied in a sheepshank knot.) Oh no! He was powerless to silence the vermin.

"What was that noise?" said the vermin in the dress and glasses.

The Black-Eyed Morgonite grunted and wagged his finger, but the vermin in the dress and glasses just kept on talking.

"Sounds like somebody's sneaking around. Uh-oh, what's the Miss gonna do when she finds out somebody snuck into His Meanness's secret lab on your watch?"

"Ayeh, euhih!" repeated the Black-Eyed Morgonite, but it was useless. The vermin in the dress and glasses wouldn't stop talking!

"Or worse, what's *His Meanness* gonna do? I bet he'll box your ears."

The Black-Eyed Morgonite frowned.

"Or tweeze all your nose hairs."

The Black-Eyed Morgonite's eyes watered. He sniffed.

"Or maybe he'll put a pebble in your shoe, and make you march around all day. Maybe you oughta go investigate!"

The Black-Eyed Morgonite nodded, raised his Magno-Baton, and was about to march off through the smoke to do just that. . . .

"Hang on!"

The Black-Eyed Morgonite stopped.

"Didn't she say 'stand right there'? Hm, that's a tough one. How are you gonna investigate *and* stand right there? I mean, if the Miss comes in, and sees you've abandoned your post . . ."

The Black-Eyed Morgonite slumped. His brain was starting to hurt.

"Maybe I can help!"

"Hmh?" The Black-Eyed Morgonite's scowl lifted slightly.

"How about if you stay put, and I go investigate for you? I'm real good at investigating stuff. Look, I've got a telescope and everything."

The Morgonite scratched under his helmet, then nodded gratefully. The vermin in the dress and glasses raised its telescope, and stalked off to investigate.

Lily tiptoed through the red smoke, ducked behind the Dejuvenation™ chair bolted to the floor, past the Dejuvenator™ Actuator, still rattling on its metal cart. She crouched against the Mean-Man's huge slab of a desk.

The butterflies in her stomach were starting to die down. Was it Kosmo she had seen through the smoke? How could it be? He was a goner, spinning like a top across the galaxy. And even if he wasn't, there was no way he was going to come *here*, to the Tower of Morgo, just to rescue—

A small, gloved hand yanked her to the floor. There, under the Mean-Man's desk, she found herself face-to-face with Kosmo Kidd. His uniform was scorched around the edges, and he smelled like a trash can.

Lily couldn't contain a happy giggle.

"Sh-sh! Keep a lid on it, mate!" whispered Kosmo. "This is a rescue mission."

"I thought you were a goner!" Lily whispered.

"Oy! I'm Kosmo Kidd, ain't I?" He took off his glove and massaged his palm.

"What's wrong with your hand?" Lily asked.

"Oh, nothing. A bit chafed, is all. From that . . . *comet*."

"What comet?"

"The comet I hitched to come save you."

"You hitched a comet?"

"Aye, nothing to it, really. Landing's a bit tricky, though. Rubbish bin broke my fall." Lily watched him pick a scrap of orange peel out of his hair, and it dawned on her that *Outer* Outer Space hadn't sent her a shooting star after all. It had sent her Kosmo Kidd. She grabbed his hand, and kissed his palm. Kosmo yanked his hand away, and stared at her, stunned.

"It's supposed to make it feel better," Lily explained.

"Oh," said Kosmo. "Well, in that case, give us another one, will ya, rookie? er—Lily?"

"The Mean-Man will be back any minute," she said. "How do we get out?"

"Same way I got in." He pointed to a floor vent against the wall, with a section of grate popped out of place. He peeked out from under the desk—seeing the Black-Eyed Morgonite facing the other direction, he started to crawl toward the open vent.

"Hang on," said Lily, holding him back by his belt. "We're gonna stick out like a sore thumb."

"So?"

"So, I got an idea. Stay put!" She tiptoed back across the room, toward the Black-Eyed Morgonite.

Kosmo reached into the pouch on his belt and took out his yellow crayon. . . .

The Black-Eyed Morgonite stood at attention. Someone tapped his back, and he whipped around.

"Easy there, fella!" said the vermin in the dress and glasses. "Oooh, that dirty sneak's gotta be around here somewhere. Don't worry, I'm hot on his trail, I just know it. Say . . ." The vermin looked down at its frilly dress and bare feet, and frowned. "If anybody catches me looking like this, they'll know you let me walk around. Boy, I'd hate for you to get in trouble, after the day you've had!"

The Black-Eyed Morgonite nodded in agreement.

"Maybe you oughta lend me that uniform of yours," suggested the vermin in the dress and glasses.

The Black-Eyed Morgonite thought it over. . . .

As he removed his helmet and cloak, and handed over his Magno-Baton, it occurred to him that these vermin might not be such terrible creatures after all.

CHAPTER 24

Oobly-eye, Oobly-oo

The walls of Morgo echoed with the chants of the Morgonites, waddling in tidy, single-file lines, until one oddly shaped Morgonite came bumping and swaying through the halls, busting up their ranks. He was lumpy and lopsided under his billowing gray cloak, teetering like a drunkard. His face was weird too, round and undersized, so that his helmet kept slipping down. If it weren't for the horn-rimmed glasses propping it up, the helmet would have covered his face

completely. The fingertips of his red gloves dangled, as if the hands inside were very small, and his Magno-Baton looked like it was ready to slip out of his grip. And what was wrong with his voice? His *Oobly-Eyes* and *Oobly-Oos* were high-pitched and squeaky.

Every Morgonite who laid eyes on him had the same thought: that he was probably ill, and badly in need of help. And since Morgonites aren't known for their sweetness, this guaranteed that they would all look the other way, and give the weird, lumpy Morgonite a wide berth.

CHAPTER 25

Mark of the Brat

Miss Meniscus caught up with the Mean-Man of Morgo outside the Big Red Door. The disappointing discovery down in the Juvy Pound had put him in a foul mood, but what better way to cheer him up than a nice Dejuvenation™?

The Big Red Door hissed open, they marched in, and there stood the Black-Eyed Morgonite, shivering in his undershorts and T-shirt, dutifully guarding an empty room.

His Meanness didn't bother chastising the brute—that sort of thing required his full attention, and right now there was a vermin on the loose. The twitch of his whiskers led him to the disturbed grate in the floor.

"Hmm, clever little brat, must have scurried out through the vent."

Miss Meniscus did not respond. Her catlike eyes were fixed on His Meanness's desk.

"What is it?" asked His Meanness.

"Nothing!" said Miss Meniscus, leaning on the desk to block his view.

He brushed her aside. What he saw there made his eyes blaze white and his whiskers sizzle. Scrawled in yellow crayon were the words:

CHAPTER 26

Escape?

The lumpy, lopsided Morgonite teetered past his stand-offish coworkers into an elevator at the end of the hall, where he finally lost his balance and toppled headlong inside. The door hissed shut behind him, and every Morgonite in the hall breathed a sigh of relief that the oddball was finally out of sight and out of mind.

The Magno-Baton clacked onto the elevator floor, the empty helmet rolled, and the cloak fell in a billowing gray heap, finally settling on the outlines of two small bodies.

Lily peered out from under the cloak. "Coast is clear!"

Kosmo peered out from under the cloak. "Time to scram! But we'll need some transportation."

"I remember a big room full of ships." Lily stood up, and looked at a map on the wall, with paths crisscrossing all through the tower. "'Hangar Bay,' that's gotta be it." She pushed a button, and the route lit up on the map.

The elevator car dropped so suddenly that she and Kosmo both flew into the air. It zipped left, then right, then down. . . .

They had almost gotten used to the feeling, when the car jerked to a halt. An alarm shrieked, and the lights began strobing red. Another staticky screen appeared, projected in midair. This time Lily saw the coiling mustache emblem of Morgo. Words scrolled by at the bottom of the screen: THE FOLLOWING IS AN URGENT MESSAGE FROM HIS MEANNESS THE MEAN-MAN OF MORGO. . . .

The alarm went quiet, the lights went dark, and on the screen, the blood-red face of the Mean-Man of Morgo appeared.

"Attention all Morgonites!" he began. "Look sharp! We have a couple of bees in our bonnet: one star-bellied

Spacetronaut, and one bespectacled *female* human. Find them, and deliver them to me, whole."

Then His Meanness leaned in so close to the screen that Lily felt the hot breath from his nostrils.

"Behold, tiny demons!" he hissed. "I believe this belongs to you. . . ." With one hand he pinched his nostrils shut, and with the other, he picked up Alfie by the scruff of his onesie.

"Alfie!" cried Lily.

"Argos!" cried Kosmo.

"If you'd like me to spare your malodorous little comrade, come forth and receive your due discipline. It won't be cake and ice cream, but you will leave here *intact*. If you refuse, I will scour this tower from top to bottom, and when I find you, your punishment will be of a more . . . *permanent nature*. So, unless you wish to feel the full vigor of my sting, I suggest you both meet me at Skydock A, upon the stroke of . . ." He pushed aside his gauntlet, to look at his wristwatch. "Seven forty-three. Over and out!"

The screen rippled and vanished. The lights came back on, and the elevator resumed its descent. Lily searched the controls. . . .

"Skydock A . . . Skydock A . . . Aha!" She pressed a button. The car screeched to a halt, flattening her and Kosmo against the floor, then shot upward.

"What are you doing?" asked Kosmo.

"We've gotta go get Argos! I mean, Alfie!"

"His Royal Redness will gut us like fish!" He slapped the Hangar Bay button. The car jerked to a stop, and flew downward again.

"He said he'd let us go."

"And you buy that, do you?"

"Well, what else can we do? I can't just let the Mean-Man have him." She hit the controls, the car stopped, and shot upward again.

"I'll tell you what else we can do: steal us a starship and skedaddle!"

Lily narrowed her eyes at Kosmo so coldly, that he shrank inside himself.

"What! You think I don't want to go save old Argos, after all the times he's saved my neck? Of course I do! But this is the Mean-Man of bleeding Morgo we're talking about!"

"All right already." Lily pushed a red button shaped like a stop sign, and the elevator scraped to a complete stop. "Why are you so afraid of the Mean-Man of Morgo?"

"Fine, I'll tell you. He . . . He spa-*nfftmh*—" He put his gloved hands over his face. Lily pulled them away.

"He what?"

"HE SPANKED ME!" His words echoed off the walls.

"Gosh," said Lily, wishing she had a better expression handy.

"Aye. Me, Kosmo Kidd, Juvenile of Juveniles, spanked! One minute we're on Planet Moltar, His Meanness and me, having your normal everyday duel to the death, when suddenly my ray gun goes dead—turns out ol' Gernsback forgot to charge the bleeding thing. Well, His Meanness gets the upper hand, and what does he do? Freeze me with his Ice Ray? Or feed me to the Great Magma Worm of Moltar, like any decent space villain would? No! He lays me across his knee . . . and . . ." Tears welled up in his eyes. "I'm no chicken. Spacetronaut's honor, I'm not."

"I know."

"You do?"

"Of course! That's why there's just one thing to do."

"Uh-oh. What's that?" asked Kosmo.

"Go look the Mean-Man in the eye, and tell him, once and for all . . ."

"Tell him what?"

"Nobody spanks Kosmo Kidd."

"Aye, nobody!"

"Nobody spanks Kosmo Kidd!" shouted Lily.

"Nobody spanks Kosmo Kidd!" Kosmo repeated.

"Like you mean it!" said Lily.

"NOBODY SPANKS KOSMO KIDD!" snarled Kosmo. He pounded the controls, and the car hurtled up the elevator shaft.

CHAPTER 27

Showdown at Skydock A

In the Murky Way, every third cycle, between the hours of seven and eight p.m., the three suns of Ophos align. Their rays collide with the red vapors of the nebula, and ignite a prismatic pinwheel of radiant sky fire. And in all of Morgo, there is no better place to view this spectacle than from the Mean-Man of Morgo's personal terrace on Skydock A. So, say what you will about His Meanness— he did know how to choose a dramatic backdrop for a climax.

Two rows of Morgonites formed a path to the end of the terrace, where the Mean-Man stood, with a wheel of fire at his back, and the Sidearm Dejuvenator™ tucked in a holster on his hip. To his right stood the Black-Eyed Morgonite (in a fresh uniform), his knees buckling under the strain of the gigantic Dejuvenator™ Actuator strapped to his back, powering His Meanness's pistol by way of its long, coiled cable. And to the Mean-Man's left stood Miss Meniscus, holding Alfie, dangling in a net.

DING! An elevator door hissed open, and at seven

forty-three on the dot, out stepped Lily Lupino. She stared down the path between the Morgonites at the Mean-Man of Morgo. He looked at his wristwatch.

"Right on time, vermin!" he shouted across the terrace.

"I want my brother back!" Lily shouted.

"I believe I was quite clear. I called for *two* troublesome vermin, yet I see only one of you. Where's your wee cohort?"

Kosmo peered out of the elevator, then slowly stepped out onto the terrace, and stood next to Lily. The door hissed shut behind him. At the sight of the Spacetronaut, the Mean-Man's mustache rippled, and his eyes twinkled with cruelty. He snapped his fingers, and the Morgonites closed in behind Lily and Kosmo.

"Charge the Actuator!" cried the Mean-Man. The Black-Eyed Morgonite flipped a switch, and the Dejuvenator™ Actuator on his back began to rattle and glow.

"Hey!" shouted Lily. "You said you'd let us go!"

"Oh, and I will, just as soon as you've had your medicine!"

"See, what did I tell you?" groaned Kosmo under his breath.

"Hmm? What was that?" shouted His Meanness. "Don't you know it's rude to whisper?"

162

Lily cupped her hand, whispered something in Kosmo's ear, and patted him on the back. Kosmo puffed up his chest, put his fists on his hips—growing a few inches before Lily's eyes—and from deep in his belly, he hollered across the terrace:

"NOBODY SPANKS KOSMO KIDD!"

The Mean-Man half smiled, half sneered, coiling his finger through his mustache. Miss Meniscus tittered.

"So . . . ," the Mean-Man began, sauntering across the terrace toward Lily and Kosmo. "Here you are at last, Spacetronaut. I was beginning to think that latest chastening I gave you back on Planet Moltar had scared you off for good." (This probably sounds familiar. His Meanness figured it was a perfectly good speech, so why let it go to waste?) "Yet here you are, bless you, shivering like a trapped rat, as the curtain draws back for the final act of our galactic pas de deux! Now, Kosmo Kidd, look on me, ye naughty, and—"

The Dejuvenator™ pistol was suddenly yanked out of his holster by its cable, which was stretched to its full length. The pistol landed—*clackity-clack*—on the floor. As the Mean-Man bent over to pick it up, he caught Lily and Kosmo smirking.

"What are you two grinning at!" he shouted, and slid the pistol back into its holster. "Where was I? Oh yes. Look on me, ye naughty and—"

Lily's and Kosmo's smiles turned into giggles.

"Cease your snickering!"

But Lily and Kosmo couldn't, or wouldn't, contain their laughter.

"What's wrong with them?" the Mean-Man asked. "Why aren't they terrified?" Miss Meniscus shrugged, wide-eyed, as Alfie, in his net, began to giggle as well. Soon even a few Morgonites were making low, clucking sounds that almost sounded like laughter.

"So be it, brats!" roared the Mean-Man, drawing the Devunator™ pistol. "This should curtail those tiresome titters. We'll start with the *female*. Restrain the specimen!" The Morgonites separated Lily and Kosmo. Two Morgonites held Lily in place, and Lily stared down the Dejuvenator's™ glowing nozzle.

"Time to grow up, little vermin!" said the Mean-Man. He pulled the trigger.

Lily shut her eyes as neon green light sliced through the air, pounded her in the chest, and nearly knocked her off her feet. Her stomach did a somersault inside her, her teeth froze, and every nerve in her body sang out in a minor key.

When she finally dared to open her eyes, the Morgonites were all staring at her, confused. Across the terrace, where the Mean-Man had been standing, there was a column of smoke.

Lily looked down at where the beam had hit her. In the middle of her mirror sash, there was a sizzling black spot. She tilted the sash to get a look at her reflection, afraid she would see a long, gray, scowling face. But there, instead, was her own round little face, looking back at her.

"Where's the Mean-Man?" whispered Kosmo.

Through the smoke, Lily could barely see the outline of a small figure, standing next to Miss Meniscus.

"And who's that little red fella?" asked Kosmo.

The smoke cleared, and Lily saw a boy, maybe a little younger than her, with a blood-red face, and wearing His Meanness's gray uniform. It was way too big for him, so that it rippled around his wrists and ankles. His eyes sparkled on the verge of tears.

"I think that little red fella *is* the Mean-Man!" whispered Lily.

"Eh? How's that work?"

"The mirror must've backwardized the beam, and turned the *De*-juvenator™ into a *Re*-juvenator!"

Lying on the red boy's oversize shoes, there was something black and spindly, twitching like a dying insect: the mustache of the Mean-Man of Morgo. He picked it up, held it to his upper lip . . . But when he let go, it fluttered back to the floor. He tried again. Again it fluttered to the floor.

His chin went dimply. He wrapped his tiny arms around Miss Meniscus's legs, buried his face in her jodhpurs, and sobbed.

"Er . . . Sire?" she sneered, and raised her gloved hand, ready to swat the child away, before he contaminated her with his juvenile face fluids. Instead, she found

166

her hand patting his little back. "There, there, little ver-min," she said, and before she knew what she was doing, she had scooped the weeping, Rejuvenated Mean-Man off his feet, leaving Alfie, in his net, on the floor.

Lily and Kosmo tiptoed across the terrace, between two rows of bewildered Morgonites, standing still as stat-ues. Alfie's piggish eyes smiled at Lily. She slipped the net off him, scooped him up, and hugged him, harder than she ever had. Then she took his hand, and she, Kosmo, and Alfie tiptoed back toward the elevator.

"Halt!" called Miss Meniscus, cradling His Formerly Meanness against her hip. He whispered in her ear, and she carried the boy toward Lily and Kosmo.

"Stay sharp!" Kosmo whispered. "Him being small doesn't make him friendly!"

"His Meanness has something he'd like to say," said Miss Meniscus. The boy hid his face in her armpit. "Now, now! Who's a shy boy! Let's just get it over with, shall we?"

His Formerly Meanness wiped his eyes. "Sorry," he said.

Lily waited a moment.

"Is that it?"

"I'm sorry, deeply sorry, for trying to Dejuvenate™ you."

"Twice," Lily reminded him.

"Twice. Of course. And I'm sorry for calling you names, like vermin, and brat. And I'm very, *very* sorry for trying to take over *Outer* Outer Space, and turn it into my own tot-free empire."

"You promise not to do anymore Dejuvenating™?" asked Lily.

The boy nodded.

"And you promise to Rejuvenate all your Morgonites back to their kid selves?"

He nodded.

"And try not to be so mean all the time!"

"I promise."

"Cross your eyes, stub your toes, stick a spindle up your nose?"

"Cross my eyes, stub my toes, stick a spindle up

168

my nose," swore His Formerly Meanness. Lily caught Miss Meniscus rolling her eyes at this sacred oath, then quickly pretending she had something in her eye.

Lily turned to Kosmo. "Satisfied?"

"Oh, nearly, nearly," he answered coldly.

"What do you mean, 'nearly'?"

"Well, there is *one thing* needling me," said Kosmo.

"Oh, rats." Lily guessed where this was headed.

"Aye, one *wee* little wrong, begging to be righted, hmmm?" And when he *hmmm*ed, his voice went high like a slide whistle. Lily saw something wispy and black on the floor next to Kosmo's foot. . . .

"Name it," said His Formerly Meanness.

"Well," Kosmo purred, "I know one little lad who's about due for . . ." A wicked grin spread across his face, and there was venom in his voice. ". . . *a spanking.*" Lily alone saw the Mean-Man's mustache tickling its way up Kosmo's ankle. "Fair's fair! Now come on down, lad, and get what's coming to you." There was fire in Kosmo's eyes as he rubbed his hands together.

"You little beast!" yelled Miss Meniscus. The red boy whimpered, and buried his face in her neck. "You dare to threaten—"

"No!" shouted Lily, and stomped the mustache under her bare foot. It gave a tiny screech, a last desperate twitch, then fell limply onto the floor. "He was

169

just kidding." She turned to Kosmo. "Weren't you?"

Kosmo's head went woozy, swaying, as the wickedness drained out of his eyes. "Aye, Your Redness. Just pulling your leg. No hard feelings!"

Lily picked up the mustache between her thumb and forefinger. "Can I have this?"

His Formerly Meanness winced. "Please! Those hateful hairs have brought me nothing but woe!" He whispered to Miss Meniscus, and she set him down. He took off his oversize gauntlet, and stuck out a red hand for Kosmo to shake. Kosmo stared at it.

"Go on!" whispered Lily, giving him a nudge. Kosmo took off his glove, but he did *not* shake the boy's hand. What he did do was perform the top-secret, Spacetronaut's-only, three-part Spacetronaut Salute.

His Formerly Meanness stared, pondering the gesture.

Finally, before the eyes of his Morgonites, and with a pinwheel of fire in the sky behind him, His Formerly Meanness performed the Spacetronaut Salute, getting it just right on his first try, even the ending with the finger blasting skyward like a rocket, while mouthing the *fffwoosh* of the engine.

As the Black-Eyed Morgonite watched Lily, Kosmo, and Alfie walk back across the terrace, he felt the corners of his mouth being pulled up and to the sides, as if by invisible hooks. . . .

CHAPTER 28

Return to Fort Spacetronaut

Davy woke up to the sound of creeping feet creaking across the floor toward the High Command Chair. Then came the familiar squeak of someone climbing up its rusty railing. He opened his eyes and sat up. . . .

Kosmo's chair wasn't empty anymore! There was a boy sitting in it, kicking his dangling feet. Davy's heart fluttered. He rubbed his eyes. Could it really be . . . ?

No. It was Pando.

Davy sprang to his feet. "What in star-nation do you reckon yer doin'?" he shouted. "That chair is the 'sclusive property of Kosmo Kidd!" In seconds, his shouting had all the Spacetronauts in the fort sitting up, yawning, stretching, and scratching.

"Kosmo Kidd has gone *adios, vaquero,*" answered Pando. "*Esta bailando con las estrellas.* I see no reason why this very comfy chair should remain *desocupado.*"

"And how do you figger you're worthy to occupy the High Command Chair?"

"Why, the reason is plain, no?" said Pando, proudly massaging his painted-on mustache.

"Hogwash! That moo-stachio ain't even for real!"

"Oh, but it is! I have very mature follicles for a boy my age."

"Are you gonna climb outta that chair, or do I hafta take ya by the ankle, and yank ya down m'self?" Davy marched to the foot of the chair. The other Spacetronauts followed him, hooting and whistling.

"Ha!" scoffed Pando. "I would enjoy to see you try, hayseed!"

"Hayseed?" gasped Davy, spitting in his palms. "Why, you duded-up *Don Juanito*!"

At that, Pando hopped down from the chair, and the two began to circle each other, with fists raised.

"Lads!" said Gernsback, inserting himself between them. "There is no call! For hostility! Let us sit down. And discuss this."

"Outta the way, Gernsy!" Davy shoved the gadgetician aside. "I'm fixin' to serve up that swarthy Spaniard a fistful o' humility!"

"I am game, *hijo de cabra*!" sneered Pando.

Davy and Pando had nearly come to blows, when Gernsback's eyes rolled madly in their sockets and he shouted, "Shame! Shame!"

Davy and Pando separated.

"And you call yourselves. Spacetronauts," said Gernsback. "Space *chimps*, more like! Sirs. You dishonor. Those stars. Upon your tummies. With your brawling. And bigotry. Shame!" He shook his head. "Shame."

"Gernsy," said Davy, lowering his fists. "I reckon you couldn't be righter if your name was Left and you was lookin' in a mirror." He wiped his hand on his onesie, and extended it to Pando. "Señor, please accept my apology."

"Likewise, *vaquero*." Pando took the frontiersman in a hearty hug. "No one wrangles the stars like Davy C. Rocket." He held his toque to his breast, and gazed upon the empty High Command Chair. "I suppose I simply could not bear to see it empty."

"By my stars, fellers," Davy said. "I got a gut fulla guilt, and it's burnin' me up inside! Why, I'd singe my fringe just to have my best friend home again." He held his coonskin cap to his breast.

Gernsback held his ball cap to his breast, and all the Spacetronauts joined in a moment of silence, looking at the empty chair. They were seconds from breaking Spacetronaut Rule Number Six—*NO BLUBBERIN'*—when they heard a deep rumble tearing through the forest outside, snapping branches as it drew nearer.

"Hit the deck!" cried a Spacetronaut in lizard-skin breeches, as a huge rectangular block of cement smashed through the wall, shaking Fort Spacetronaut from root to twig. It had a glowing, domed windshield, and a fin on its back. Its engine faded to a low hum.

"A Morgo. Star Skiff," observed Gernsback. "Or I'm. A Monkey. Zuncle."

A door in the side hissed open, and out stepped a boy-shaped shadow, coughing, waving away the dust that danced like fireflies in the windshield's light.

"Fellers!" whispered Davy. "Either it's time I start believin' in spirits, or that there's Kosmo Kidd, in the flesh."

Gernsback closed one eye, and with the other, scanned the silhouette. "Life Functions..."—*DING!*—"Positive!" The Spacetronauts crowded in and embraced Kosmo.

"Koz!" yelled Davy. "We figgered you were off kickin' the bucket!"

"Joining! The choir invisible!" added Gernsback.

"*¡Criando malvas!*" added Pando.

"Did I not say you ain't seen the last o' me?" said Kosmo.

"You surely did," answered Davy. "And we never shoulda figgered otherly-wise. And let me be the first to tell ya how sorely tore up we all was at havin' zapped you away. It was most foolish and unspacemanly."

"All in the rear view, lads," answered Kosmo.

"I mean, what good's a rule pits brother 'gainst brother, anyhow?"

"Hear, hear!" said many.

"Well, it's good you say that, lads," said Kosmo. "'Cause you'll never guess who I brung back—"

The Spacetronauts cheered and whistled at the sight (but not the smell) of Alfie, toddling out of the ship. (None of them let on that, until that moment, they hadn't noticed the toddler was missing.)

"Aye," said Kosmo. "Our own dear Agent Argos, back once again from the brink of doom. But also . . ." He cupped his hand and shouted, "It's all right, come on out!"

Another silhouette peered out of the skiff. For a better look, Davy waved away the dust with his cap. . . .

"Botheration!" he cursed. "Not again."

CHAPTER 29

Foregone Whiskers

"Fellers, flank that filly!" said Davy, and the Spacetronauts surrounded Lily. "Koz, looks like this here vix-*een* musta stowed away on you."

"I did not!" Lily shouted.

"*¡Silencio!*" hissed Pando. "You will not poison us with your lies."

"It's no lie! Tell 'em, Kosmo," said Lily.

"Yeah, Koz, tell us!" Davy put an arm around Kosmo, and said, confidentially, "Now, Koz, I know you done learned yer lesson by now."

"That I have, Davy. That I have."

"Darn tootin'! Then all you need say is that this here she-spy got the jump on ya, and we'll give 'er the ol' one-boot salute, and be back to business as regular!"

"Aye, lads!" said Kosmo, loud enough for all to hear. "I've learned me a thing or two, such as: Maybe females ain't so unfit for space after all."

"Oh yeah, Koz?" pressed Davy. "How ya figger?"

"Oy, Lupino, show the lads how I figger," said Kosmo.

Lily held her souvenir high for all the fort to see. Every Spacetronaut in the fort gasped to see those legendary whiskers.

"*¡Madre de Fuego*," whispered Pando, "*el bigote!*"

"As I rope and ride," uttered Davy, "the lady done nabbed it!"

"Aye, from under His Meanness's very nose," said Kosmo, "and right-bravely, eh, Lupino?"

"Right-bravely," agreed Lily.

Held high, the mustache began to move. First it was a gentle quiver, then an angry thrashing. Lily saw the lights in Fort Spacetronaut dim, and the Spacetronauts shrinking at her feet. Their eyes were wide with admiration. Or was it fear? Whatever it was, it felt good! No one could ever tell Lily Lupino she could or couldn't be this or that, because she wasn't this or that. No one would dare to mess with her molly-cules ever again. She'd like to see them try, the little *vermin*! Fort Spacetronaut and its puny inhabitants became a faraway blur, as the mustache pulled itself like a magnet toward her face, groping for her upper lip. . . .

"I know a better spot for them whiskers, mate."

The whisper found her ear, and Kosmo came into focus, handing her a hammer and nail. Lily shook her woozy head, and Fort Spacetronaut and all its Spacetronauts reappeared.

She and Kosmo marched over to the Mishun Controll Centr. Lily climbed onto Kosmo's shoulders, held up the mustache, and hammered the nail through it dead center. Then she drew a chalk line through the words NAB THE MENEMANS MOSTASH FRUMUNDR HIS VAIRY NOS.

"Mission o'complished!" Kosmo shouted. The Spacetronauts echoed the cry.

"Well, uh, ma'am," said Davy, taking off his cap, "I figger any gal who's man enough to face the Menace of the Murky Way is man enough to wear the star o' the Spacetronauts. Fellers, are we agreed on that?"

There was a chorus of yeses.

"Indeed!" answered Gernsback. "Amending bylaws . . . Stand by . . ." His eyes rolled back as his brain processed the command. "From now on. The Spacetronauts are. A co-ed. Operation." The Spacetronauts cheered for their newest recruit, except for Pando, who was staring at the floor.

"Say, cookie," said Davy, patting the troubled chef's shoulder. "What gives?"

"Lads, lady," began Pando, "there is a lie in my heart, and I must be free of it. This *mustachio* of mine, which you have all so admired"—he licked his hand, wiped it across his upper lip, and held his blackened palm up for all to see—"is a sham! A ruse!" He hung his head in shame.

The Spacetronauts all did him the favor of pretending to be shocked.

"But Lily," Pando continued, "you have taught me that it is not the whiskers on your lip that make you strong, but the whiskers in your heart. *Bienvenidos a los Spacetronauts, amigo.*"

"Ami-*ga*," Lily corrected.

"*Claro*," Pando agreed.

"Right, lads!" Kosmo shouted, climbing into the High Command Chair. "Back to work!"

CHAPTER 30

The Next Daring Mission

Gernsback brought forth the Mission Control can. Davy gave it a crank. It spat out a card, and Pando caught it. He struggled to read it, but gave up and handed it to Lily, who read: DELIVVER AJENT ARGOS BAK TO PLANNIT URTH. Out loud, she sounded it out:

"Deliver Agent Argos Back to Planet Earth."

"Huh? Hang on a tick!" said Davy, grabbing the card from her. "How'd this 'un get in thar?" He looked from Spacetronaut to Spacetronaut. "Did *you* put this in thar? Or *you*?" But all he got were shaking heads. "Well, somebody done wrote it!"

Ahem!

Some deep-voiced fellow had cleared his throat. But who? The Spacetronauts turned to the balcony. There, standing on an apple crate, was Agent Argos.

"Dear friends," he said, in a low, smooth voice that belonged on the radio. "It was I who wrote that mission, I who slipped it into the Mission Control Cannister."

"But Argos! How come?" asked Davy.

"Yeah, old man, how come?" asked Kosmo.

"Lads, Comrades, Spacetronauts," said Argos, pacing the balcony. "Though the road of a spaceman is fraught with trials, it is as rich a calling as a man could hope to find. I speak not of a wealth measured in whiskers and lizard tails—oh no!—but in the bonds of a sacred brotherhood, forged in the eternal flame of cosmic struggle."

Lily's jaw dropped, hearing these grand words coming from the two-year-old's mouth. But she was the only one; the rest of the Spacetronauts were listening, with sadness in their eyes.

"Now," Argos continued. "I turn my gaze toward the beckoning sunset of retirement, bolstered by the knowledge that Lily Lupino, my savior and successor, will bring great honor to the continuing legacy of . . . *the Spacetronauts!*"

"But Argos!" Kosmo protested. "They're bleeding savages, Earth Men. You'll be locked up again, like an animal behind bars!"

183

"Savages?" answered Argos. "Perhaps. But their sheets are soft, and they know how to change a diaper." He turned to his one-legged velveteen pig. "Well, Colonel? Shall we stroll those greener pastures together?"

Colonel Shanks voiced no objections.

"Well, lads," Kosmo announced, "looks like I'm earthbound once again. Anybody care to join me?" All through the fort, hands shot into the air. "Right! I'll take Davy C. Rocket, and . . . Oy, Pando! Have you ever had an away mission?"

Chef Pando shook his head sadly.

"Well, no better time to start," said Kosmo. Pando hopped with joy.

"That leaves room for one more." Kosmo turned to Lily. "Lupino, you'd make a right-useful navigator, being an ex-Earther yourself. What do you say?"

"Hmm . . . Can I drive?"

Kosmo smiled. "Right, crew! Gear up, and make ready for launch in . . . Uh-oh, hang on." He tapped his chin, watching Davy and Pando gleefully pick out their space helmets.

"Is it me, Lupino," said Kosmo, "or are we all looking a bit scruffy for a mission? Any chance you'd be up for giving us a preflight trim?"

CHAPTER 31

Earthbound

"All aboard!" hollered Kosmo, beaming with his freshly trimmed hair, standing beside the freshly wound Mildred. One by one, the mission crew slid down the fire pole into the hangar, each sporting a handsome new do from their new expert barber.

Zhoop—First came Davy C. Rocket, King of the Final Frontier, trimmed close around the ears and the back, but wavy on top with a nice clean part. He climbed through the hatch, into the back seat, and sat beside Agent Argos, who had Colonel Shanks on his lap.

Zhoop—Next came Pando the Chef, hair slicked straight back with a mirror sheen. He crawled in, and sat beside Davy.

And finally—*zhoop*—came Lily Lupino, Barber-Navigator. She took a look at her reflection in Mildred's windshield. Her own short and shiny do—the "Trip Darrow"—was as dapper as it was practical, and perfectly complemented the Spacetronaut star freshly stitched to the tummy of her nightgown.

Kosmo climbed in, and crawled across to the passenger seat. Lily sat in the pilot's seat, closed the hatch behind her, and buckled her seat belt. Kosmo pounded on the dashboard, and the controls blinked to life.

"Evening, Mildred!" said Lily. Mildred answered with a confused chirp.

"No, Mildred," said Kosmo. "Lupino's gonna drive." Mildred chattered in protest. In the back seat, Davy and Pando turned a little green, and buckled their seat belts.

"Well, she's got to learn sometime, eh?" said Kosmo. "Fire up scramjets and make ready for liftoff. Ten . . . Nine . . . Eight . . ." The engine whined. Their seats shook and turned hot.

Lily gripped the joystick. Through the windshield,

and through the small, square portal out of the hangar, space beckoned.

Kosmo finished his countdown: "Three . . . Two . . . One!"

Lily found a big red button on the dashboard marked IGNISHUN.

"Blastoff!" she shouted, over the engine's roar, and hit the button. "*Ffffwwooooosshhh!!*"

CHAPTER 32

Brooklyn, Earth (Revisited)

By the time they made it out of *Outer* Outer Space, through Outer Space, and all the way back to Regular Space, Lily had gotten the hang of steering the rocket, and Mildred had only one or two fresh dings to show for the journey. The stars looked puny and far away, and no longer whizzed by, so it was hard to tell if the rocket was still getting anywhere. In the back, Davy, Pando, and Agent Argos snored. In the passenger seat, Kosmo's head bobbed onto his chest.

Lily's eyelids had just begun to droop when, dead ahead, one of the stars flared up bigger and brighter than the others. It was the sun, *Lily's* sun. Scattered around it, like an abandoned game of marbles, were Pluto, Neptune, Jupiter, and the rest. The streaky blue-green marble of Earth nudged the others aside, and swelled up to fill the windshield.

Lily's guts twisted into a knot, as she pictured Mr. and Mrs. Lupino standing guard over Argos's empty crib, ready to seize her on sight. Maybe the cops would even be there too, at the scene of the crime. After all, Lily had earned herself quite a rap sheet since that little incident with the scissors. Now she was a runaway, too, a fugitive, a delinquent. And there was that giant hole in the living room ceiling—they'd probably pin *that* on her too, and the busted fridge, and maybe throw in the blown-up moon to boot. If they nabbed her now, she'd be lucky if she ever set foot outside her own *home* again, let alone her home *planet*.

"How long were we away?" Lily asked.

"What, Earth time?" said Kosmo, shaking off sleep. "Beats me. Space time runs a bit stretchier than on Earth."

Whatever that meant, it didn't make Lily feel any better. She wanted to yank the hand brake, hang a U-turn, and rocket straight back to the fort.

No!

She was a Spacetronaut, and Spacetronauts see their missions through. She steered Mildred into Earth's shadowy half, and pierced a layer of clouds, until a grid of golden lights simmered up out of the dark. She eased back on the joystick, coasting low over dim streets, spiny churches, and dark, clustered buildings. Only a few windows here and there were lit.

"Look familiar, rookie?" asked Kosmo.

"Um . . ." It didn't. Lily wasn't used to seeing Brooklyn from this angle, definitely not this far past her bedtime, and without a moon in the sky to light the way.

A wide, flat black patch slid below them, with little white squares in neat rows.

Gravestones!

It was the big, spooky graveyard across from Lily's school. She steered along Flatbush Avenue, then turned left at the fire station, and spotted her own brick building ahead.

"Mildred, make ready to land."

Mildred eased off on her thrusters, as Lily circled the rooftop in a mellow, downward spiral, aiming for the big crater in the middle of the roof, where Kosmo "landed" last time.

Why make a ruckus, punching another hole in the building?

190

"Setting down in three . . . two . . . ," said Lily, as Mildred's underbelly skimmed the rooftop, right on track for a hole-in-one landing. . . .

But a jutting pipe snagged Mildred's grille, launching her into a forward somersault right off the roof. She slammed against the trunk of an old maple, and would have dived four stories straight into the pavement, if something hadn't broken her fall; a branch caught them in its gnarled grip, sagged under the weight of five Spacetronauts and one windup tin rocket, sprang up again, and finally bobbed to rest outside a dark, top-floor window.

Lily opened Mildred's hatch. There, at the end of the gently bobbing branch, were the gauzy curtains of her very own bedroom.

"All in once piece back there?" she asked, but the back seat Spacetronauts

had barely lifted an eyelid; this was a smoother landing than they were used to.

"Rise and shine, lads!" shouted Kosmo. "Time for Operation Nappy Drop. Pando! Davy C.!" Pando and Davy sprang up in their seats, ready for action. "You two flank the window. Lupino, you ready 'the Package' for delivery," said Kosmo, nodding toward Argos. "Me, I'll scout ahead for unfriendlies." Smiling his wolfish smile, he drew his ray gun.

"Maybe I should deliver the Package alone," Lily suggested.

"Aye, a stealth mission. Good call," agreed Kosmo— only a little let down to have to holster his ray gun. "Davy and Pando, sit tight." Davy and Pando were already nodding off again.

Lily unfastened her seat belt, and shimmied across the branch, trying to ignore the four-story drop below her. She tugged at the window frame, but it wouldn't budge.

"Locked!" she whispered.

"Fear not!" answered Kosmo, tossing her his ray gun. Lily fired a quick pulse through the glass, melting the latch into a hissing, glowing puddle, then tossed the ray gun back to Kosmo. She slid the window open, peeked through the parted curtain, and gave her eyes a couple seconds to adjust. There was no one inside, and the room looked just as she'd left it. Her bedcovers were still rumpled, from where she hopped out of bed to investigate Kosmo's crash.

"All clear!" she whispered. "Cue the Package."

Kosmo guided Argos out of the hatch. Gripping Colonel Shanks in his mouth, Argos scooched along the branch, across Lily's lap, through the parted curtain, and into the darkened bedroom. Lily was about to hop in after him, when a horrible thought occurred to her: What if, when the curtain closed behind her, the rocket, all traces of *Outer* Outer Space, evaporated like a dream into the Brooklyn night air?

"Don't go anywhere!" she whispered. "Promise?"

"Spacetronaut's Honor," said Kosmo, with his hand on his chest. "If you run into any unfriendlies, just give a whistle!"

Lily hopped through the curtain. Argos was already half-asleep, leaning against his crib.

"You sure about this, Argos?" Lily whispered. Argos tossed Colonel Shanks into the crib, raised his arms toward Lily, and let out a drowsy whimper. She kissed the seasoned Spacetronaut's sleepy head, hugged him, and with all her might, hoisted him up over the railing. Argos flopped onto the mattress, and in three seconds flat, was fast asleep.

Click!

The room lit up, bright as day. Scowling in the doorway was Mr. Lupino, in his bathrobe, with his finger on

193

the light switch.

Lily froze, with her hands still on the railing of the crib. She puckered her lips to whistle for help, but there was no breath in her chest to push the sound out. She was caught! She had made it all the way to *Outer* Outer Space and back, only to wake up in the starlessness of her old bedroom.

"Lily Lupino!" her father growled. "Hands off the crib. Now!" Lily dropped her hands to her sides. "I don't know what's gotten into you tonight, but the next time I catch you terrorizing your poor brother . . . !"

Tonight?

There was probably more to that sentence, but Lily didn't hear anything past the word . . .

Tonight!

"What's the matter, hon?" Mrs. Lupino asked, shuffling up beside Mr. Lupino, tying her bathrobe. There were faint black stripes on her cheeks, left over from where tears had dragged mascara down her face, then dried into a crust.

Of course! Because here on Earth, it was still "tonight," *Trip Darrow* night, scissors night.

Space time runs a bit stretchier . . .

Indeed! It had stretched like a rubber band across the stars, and snapped Lily right back to the night she left.

"Nothing," answered Mr. Lupino. "Just more monkey business. Go back to bed." Mrs. Lupino did just that, and Mr. Lupino was about to follow, when something caught his eye. "What's that?"

"What's what?" asked Lily.

"That, on your nightgown."

"A star."

"Well, what's it doing on your nightgown?"

Lily shrugged.

"Tomorrow that's going right in the trash with all the other space nonsense. This astronaut baloney ends now, you hear me?" Looking at the floor, Lily nodded—anything to get him to leave, so she could make her escape!

"You're not an astronaut, are you?" said Mr. Lupino. Lily shook her head. Triumphant, Mr. Lupino switched off the light and turned to leave, but before he could pull the door shut behind him . . .

"I'm a Spacetronaut," Lily declared, because she couldn't bear not to.

Mr. Lupino turned, to find his daughter standing in the dark, meeting his scowl with a thousand-light-year-stare of her own. His scowl melted into something different, an expression Lily recognized, but couldn't put a name to, which she had only seen him give to people taller than himself.

"Bed," he managed to say, and pulled the door shut behind him.

In his crib, Agent Argos opened his eyes in time to see Lily step onto the windowsill, smile back at him, and vanish through the parted curtain. And the last thing he saw, before the deep, downy sleep of Earth took him, was the outline of Lily Lupino, Spacetronaut, standing proud with her fists on her hips. Then the night breeze rippled the curtain, and she was gone.

ACKNOWLEDGMENTS

I want to thank my literary agent, Mark Gottlieb, for inspiring, guiding, amd welcoming me into the world of publishing.

I'm grateful to my editor, David Gale, for his keen storytelling instincts, which enriched this story immeasurably.

And I'm fortunate to have worked with designer Krista Vossen, who crafted this book into a beautiful work of art.

And I owe a specal thanks to The Shelter, the theater workshop where Lily Lupino and Kosmo Kidd were born and raised. This story wouldn't exist without this warm, wise, and immensely talented family of artists.